"Are you upset to find that I'm alive?" Luke asked.

"Of course not! It's good that you survived the explosion. It's just..."

"Just what?" he prompted.

She shifted in her seat and met his gaze head-on. "I don't know you anymore. Which must sound selfish of me. I'm sorry, truly I am. I know that you have lost your memories. I can't even imagine how that must feel."

"It's disconcerting, that's for sure. It's also painful to know that I've been a father for four years and have missed it."

"I understand that." Her voice was soft. "I'm just not certain how to proceed. You're a stranger to me. And my life has finally gotten to a point where I feel like I'm moving forward. Or it was."

What had changed that more—knowing he was alive or knowing that Steve was out to get her? Steve. What were they doing sitting in a car when that man was still out there, waiting for the opportunity to attack again?

"We need to get inside. We're vulnerable here."

Dana R. Lynn grew up in Illinois. She met her husband at a wedding and told her parents she'd met the man she was going to marry. Nineteen months later, they were married. Today, they live in rural Pennsylvania with their three children and a variety of animals. In addition to writing, she works as a teacher for the deaf and hard of hearing and is active in her church.

Books by Dana R. Lynn

Love Inspired Suspense

Amish Country Justice

Plain Target
Plain Retribution
Amish Christmas Abduction
Amish Country Ambush
Amish Christmas Emergency
Guarding the Amish Midwife
Hidden in Amish Country
Plain Refuge
Deadly Amish Reunion

Visit the Author Profile page at Harlequin.com.

DEADLY AMISH REUNION

DANA R. LYNN

LOVE INSPIRED SUSPENSE
INSPIRATIONAL ROMANCE

LOVE INSPIRED® SUSPENSE

INSPIRATIONAL ROMANCE

ISBN-13: 978-1-335-40321-6

Recycling programs
for this product may
not exist in your are

Deadly Amish Reunion

Love Inspired
22 Adelaide St. West, 40th Floor
Toronto, Ontario M5H 4E3, Canada
www.Harlequin.com

Printed in U.S.A.

But seek ye first the kingdom of God,
and his righteousness; and all these things
shall be added unto you.
        –Matthew 6:33

For my children

ONE

Where had he seen that face before?

Luke Beiler frowned at the face on the television news report behind the front counter. He knew that man. The scowling face with the angry eyes sent chills of foreboding down his spine. Whoever he was, he was dangerous.

Luke focused on the captioned words below the picture. Steve Curtis, aged forty-eight, in prison for rape, attempted murder and assault with a deadly weapon, had escaped from prison.

"Police warn that Steve Curtis is dangerous and very likely armed," the news anchor said into the camera. The camera shifted to a reporter standing outside the prison. "Janelle?"

"Marie, the prison isn't commenting yet as to how he managed to escape. One theory spreading through the area is that Steve Curtis didn't escape on his own. The police are asking citizens to call the number on the screen if they have any information on his whereabouts or about anyone connected with his escape. Back to you, Marie."

Marie faced the camera again. "If you see Steve Curtis, police are warning you not to approach him but call them immediately."

The news anchor began reporting on the next story, something about a series of home invasions and robberies occurring these past two weeks before Christmas. Luke tuned them out, frowning as he tried to force himself to recall anything about Steve Curtis.

"Luke, *cumme!*"

Luke pulled his mind back to the present and hefted the fifty-pound bag of animal feed over his shoulder, nearly knocking over a small Christmas tree on a stand. His free hand shot out to steady the tree, then he followed his brother Raymond out of the small country store located outside of New Wilmington, Pennsylvania, their boots crunching on the December snow.

Luke's pace was slower today and his limp more pronounced. He'd been overdoing it lately. The doctor had warned him that his leg would never be as strong as it had been before he was injured.

Not that he could remember anything about that. Luke had woken up in a ditch one day, several hours away from his parents' home near New Wilmington. He had no memory of how he had gotten there. He'd been wearing a flannel shirt that had seen much better days and jeans that had been ripped to pieces. His left leg had been in agony. The last thing he remembered was being on his *rumspringa*, so he'd not thought too much about his attire.

He'd been able to hitch a ride from a farmer to his parents' *haus*. Nothing could prepare him for their shocked reaction. And he'd been even more astonished to learn that he was not seventeen, but twenty-two. His parents had informed him that he had had a fight with his father and had left in the middle of the night five years earlier. They hadn't seen or heard from him since.

They had the local doctor come and treat his leg. He'd had a partial fracture. The doctor had mused that he might have been hit by a car, but if he had been, they'd never found out who had struck him.

To this day, he had no idea what he had done in those five years.

"Luke, bist du gut?"

"Jah, Raymond. I'm *gut*. Just thinking."

"Ach. No wonder you're so slow today."

Luke grinned, but in his heart, he didn't feel it. Something dark hovered in his mind. He attempted to shrug it off and followed Raymond out to the parking lot.

Several buggies were there. New Wilmington's Amish buggies were unique, black on the bottom with burnt-orange tops. Usually, the Amish goal was not to stand out. In this one aspect, however, the nineteen districts of New Wilmington stood apart from the Amish communities in the rest of the country. Luke clambered up into the buggy beside his brother, grunting as his whole weight briefly settled on his bad leg. It was bitterly cold this morning. His breath misted in the air in front of his face, blurring his vision.

As he dropped onto the seat, an image briefly seared across his brain. And a name. "Jennie!"

"What?" Raymond flicked the reins to start the horses moving before tossing a frown at his older brother.

"I don't know." He couldn't shake the sense of urgency. "I just have an image in my mind. A girl. Long brown hair. Brown eyes. She's so familiar. I think her name is—"

"Jennie." There was an unfamiliar heaviness in his brother's voice. Raymond was made for cheer, always ready to laugh.

"You know her?" Luke asked his brother. Why would that surprise him? Raymond might be four years younger than Luke, but he had five years of memories that Luke, at twenty-seven, had lost.

"*Jah*. I know her." Raymond hesitated. "She was a friend of yours when we were working on building *hauser* with *Onkel* Jed." Their *onkel* Jed lived near Spartansburg, a rural area nearly seventy miles north of where the rest of his family lived. In Luke's mind, he could visualize his *daed*'s twin brother. They might have looked alike, but Jed's nature was more flexible.

Luke squeezed his eyes shut, willing the image of the girl to return. "I don't remember anything about her. Why would I think of her now?" Another question struck him. "If we were such *gut* friends, why have you never mentioned her before?"

His brother shrugged but wouldn't meet his eyes. "You were home. She wasn't Plain."

Suddenly something clicked. "*Daed* worried I might have been drawn to her, didn't he?" It really wasn't a question. Luke had recalled hearing his father and mother whispering about him soon after he'd returned. They had been concerned that if he regained his memory he might wish to go back to the *Englisch* world. When his memories hadn't returned, he'd settled into the Amish world again and had even been baptized into the church two years ago.

"*Jah*, he and *Mamm* were both worried," Raymond finally responded as if the words were dragged from him.

"I have to find her." Luke hadn't planned on saying

that, but now that the words were out there, he knew it was true.

"For what reason? It's been years since you've seen her."

The picture of Steve Curtis flashed in his mind again. "That man on the news. Steve Curtis. He's a bad man, with plenty of reason to hate Jennie. He'll hurt her." *Again.* Luke didn't question how he knew that the man had hurt the girl before, just as he didn't question the desperation crawling inside him, making him itch from the inside out. He didn't remember much about Jennie, not even her last name. But she was important to him. And she was in trouble. Deadly trouble.

Raymond tried to convince him to let it go all the way home, but Luke dug in his heels. He couldn't ignore the girl that hovered on the fringes of his memory. Not when he thought she was in danger.

Although, he strongly suspected her image would disturb him even if he wasn't sure she was in harm's way.

"She's in danger, Ray. I have to find her. You can help me or not, but don't think you can stop me."

He bore his brother's appraising gaze in silence, jaw clenched. He would not, could not, budge on this issue.

"*Ach*, you always were stubborn. Fine. I will go with you. Let's empty the buggy, then we can leave."

Satisfied, Luke nodded. "I'll call to see if we can find a driver."

Raymond frowned, but didn't object. "*Jah*, if we're going to Spartansburg, it would be best."

Without another word, Luke ignored his aching leg and strode to the barn. Their bishop allowed them a phone in their businesses for such matters. It took Luke fifteen minutes to find a driver who could come on short notice, but he finally found one. He returned to the buggy and assisted his brother, carrying the heavy bags from the buggy and into the barn. When the last bag had been moved, he went into the *haus* to pack a lunch for them and gather together a change of clothes.

"How long do you plan on being gone?" Raymond asked from the doorway as he watched Luke throw the clothes into a knapsack.

. Luke shrugged. "Probably just a few hours. But I want to be prepared."

Bag packed, he moved out onto the porch to wait for the driver. Raymond explained to their mother that they were heading to Spartansburg. Luke noticed he made no mention of Jennie, whoever she was. It was probably for the best. He couldn't have explained the urgency sweeping through his veins.

When their driver, Sam, arrived, Raymond sat in the back, allowing Luke to sit up front in the passenger seat. As Sam drove, Luke stared out the window, pounding his fist lightly against his thigh.

He'd been down these roads so many times in the past five years. Now his eyes scoured the passing scenery, searching for some clue that might jog his lost memories. Just one hint about who this woman was and why his very soul screamed that he needed to hurry.

Sam pulled off I-79 at the Meadville-Conneaut Lake exit. Luke's entire body sprang to attention.

"Is something wrong?" Raymond demanded from the back.

"She's here, in Meadville. Not in the city, but close to it. At least, I think she is." How he knew this, he couldn't say. But now that they were here, he could sense that they were getting close. He couldn't visualize the whole journey or the end destination, but as they approached an intersection, he knew whether they should turn or keep straight. The streets, with their wreath-decorated light posts, were somehow familiar. He'd definitely been here before.

Part of him was excited that his memory might be returning. But most of his thoughts were consumed with the image of the brown-haired woman he'd seen in his mind. He knew she was in danger. Just as he knew she was somehow important to him, but he wasn't willing to share that insight with his brother. Not yet, with tension zipping through him, tightening his shoulders and clenching his gut.

A little more than a half hour later, he pressed his face closer to the window, staring at the scenery, the familiarity of the place like a spiderweb he'd walked under. He could feel it—it tickled his senses, but he couldn't quite grasp it.

He'd been through here many times before when he'd traveled to *Onkel* Jed and *Tante* Eleanor's *haus*. Yet never had his emotions been stirred to this extent.

He knew this place, more than just as a spectator moving through.

He had lived here, or close by. He couldn't remember anything else, but this he knew for a fact. Under his breath, he muttered a quick prayer for *Gott* to bless their endeavor.

This was where they would find Jennie.

If they weren't too late.

The phone was ringing as Jennie Beiler shoved her key into the lock of her apartment and let herself in.

"Hold on. Hold on," she muttered, kicking off her gray booties by the door before hurrying to the kitchen. She set one of the grocery bags on the counter. Then she pushed the speaker on the phone.

"Hello?"

"Hey, girl. It's Randi."

"Hold on a minute." Jennie grabbed her earbuds and pushed the plug into the audio jack. Placing the small plastic buds in her ears, she shoved the phone into her back jeans pocket. "Okay, I can hear you now."

Randi Griggs was her oldest friend. They'd known each other since they were both eleven and in foster care. They chatted for a few minutes about Christmas plans. Neither Jennie nor Randi had parents around, although they both had older brothers.

"Are you going to see your brother and his wife?" Randi asked.

Jennie washed the vegetables before putting them in the refrigerator. Her son, LJ, loved green peppers and carrots, so she always made sure to have those on hand.

"No. He and Sophie are traveling this year with Celine and their daughter." Celine was Sophie's sixteen-year-old sister.

The neighbors in the next apartment started arguing. Jennie flipped the television on and kept the volume on low to block out the words. She didn't particularly want to hear what they were fighting about.

"I'll bet LJ is still begging for a puppy," Randi laughed.

Jennie carried the milk and orange juice to the refrigerator, opening her mouth to reply, but the words lodged in her throat as she saw the television news alert.

Sudden fear choked her. Steve Curtis had escaped from prison.

She hadn't seen her stepfather since she was fifteen. Not since she'd testified against him for rape and attempted murder. He looked older, and harder, but she'd know that face anywhere. And now he was on the loose.

He would come for her. She knew it. He had promised he'd get his revenge for her costing him everything. Steve always kept his promises.

The two containers slipped from Jennie's hands. The gallon of milk burst open and splashed on her white-washed jeans and soaked her thick pink woolen socks. She ignored the discomfort. And the ruined groceries. Her world had tipped on its side and she was struggling to keep her balance.

"Jennie? Are you still there?"

Randi's voice pulled her back to the present.

Jennie squeezed her eyes shut, forcing her mind to blot out the memories assailing her. "Randi, I'm sorry. I have to go. Call you later."

Without waiting for a response, she hung up on the other woman. Her breath hitched as her anxiety spiked.

The man who had attacked her, not once but twice, had escaped from prison.

When Steve had first attacked her, she'd been barely eleven, and her brother, Aiden, had rescued her before she was harmed. Her testimony against her stepfather had put Steve in jail for attempted rape and assault.

Her mother had accused her of lying, of trying to destroy their family. Even with Aiden there as a witness, she'd refused to accept that what her children said was true. By the time she had realized her daughter was telling the truth, the system had declared her an unfit mother for endangering the welfare of her children. Jennie and Aiden were removed from the home. The mortification had been too much. Barbara Forster had divorced her worthless husband, emptied their checking account and relinquished her parental rights. Jennie never saw her again.

Aiden and Jennie had no other family. Their father had died years before. They had landed in different foster care homes. She'd always lived with the dread of Steve returning for her. She woke up, night after night, his threats ringing in her ears. She was to blame for the loss of his wife, his job and his reputation. Because of her, he would forever be branded a predator. Her fears had become a reality when she was fifteen, and Steve had gotten out on parole after serving less than four years. He'd come after her, just like he'd promised. Without her brother around, he'd violently assaulted her and stabbed her in the shoulder.

Luke had heard her screaming. He'd arrived too late to save her from being raped, but he was in time to save her life. He'd grabbed the knife before Steve could stab her a second time. Once again, she testified against Steve, this time for rape and attempted murder.

Luke had been wonderful. He'd stayed with Jennie during her therapy, brought her wounded heart back to life. When she was nineteen, she'd married him. They were young, but she felt what they had would last forever. She had dropped her defenses and allowed herself to love. Then he'd been killed in an explosion at work five years ago. His body had never been recovered.

Needing something to occupy herself, Jennie grabbed the mop from the closet to clean up the mess from the spilled milk. Her hands shook as she turned on the faucet. A rock sat in the pit of her stomach, unsettling the bagel she'd indulged in earlier while running errands.

Images from the past kept intruding. Steve's face, dark with anger above her. His fist coming down fast. Luke telling her he loved her, that he'd never leave her.

But he had left her, although not by choice.

She dashed her fist across her eyes, swiping away the wetness.

She was so done crying. He had sworn he'd never leave, and then he was gone. Three others had been killed in the explosion, and their wives had been able to bury them.

She'd buried an empty casket.

And her heart.

Well, not completely.

Jennie finished cleaning the floor and put the mop away, touching a picture on the wall as she passed. Luke Junior, or LJ, had curly blond hair, blue eyes and a smile that could melt stone. The one thing that remained of the love she'd shared with Luke. The reason she was able to get up each morning and smile.

"Oh, no!" Shock rooted her feet to the floor. What if Steve went after him? What if he targeted her son to get his revenge? LJ was only four. He'd been taught not to talk to strangers, but he was still only a small child. No match for a man like Steve.

It was a good thing she'd taken the day off for a dental appointment. Jennie worked as a computer technician Monday through Thursday, but her dentist was closed on Fridays. If she'd been at work, she probably would have missed the alert about Steve.

She grabbed her keys and hurried to the door, brushing against the Christmas tree. A handful of ornaments tumbled to the tree skirt. She ignored them as she ran to the small shoe mat near the door and shoved her feet into her booties. She didn't even take the time to lock the door. LJ's preschool didn't end for another hour, but she couldn't wait. She needed to hold her baby in her arms now, to see for herself that he was well. Safe.

She dashed down the steps at top speed, nearly colliding with another tenant. She didn't know his name, only that he worked nights and she rarely saw him. He wobbled on the stairs.

"Sorry!" she yelled, continuing her mad dash to get her son.

Once outside, she had to slow down, although she didn't want to. The landlord hadn't spread salt on the icy walk yet. The path between the apartment building and the parking lot was slick enough to sled on. Meadville and the surrounding area was part of the northwestern PA snowbelt, so they got pelted frequently with snow and ice. After what felt like forever, she made it to her car and buckled herself in.

The temptation to pray for safety for herself and her son hit her in a wave so hard, she rocked in her seat. She shrugged it off. God wouldn't help her. Where was He all those hard years? If He had loved her, shouldn't He have protected her? She couldn't get beyond her bitterness.

At least she had LJ. She'd also found her brother, Aiden, again. He'd located her four and a half years ago. If only Aiden were home, she and LJ would go and stay with him. But he wasn't. He and Sophie had taken a trip to France for the holidays with their three-year-old daughter, Rose, and Celine. They'd invited Jennie and her son, but Jennie had declined. She'd never been on a plane before and wasn't comfortable with her first flight being across the ocean. She was now regretting that decision. Had she gone with them, Aiden would have been with her when she heard of Steve's escape. He would have known what to do.

She couldn't lose focus. The preschool was ten minutes away normally, but the icy conditions doubled her time. What if she was too late? If she lost LJ, she'd never survive it.

Shifting her car into Park with enough force that the engine shuttered, she turned off the ignition and threw the door open. She hurried past a man dressed like Santa. Her eyes briefly met his as he waved at those passing and called out Christmas greetings. She averted her eyes, tensing. Ridiculous to be scared of a man trying to drum up business for his store. Still, something about him unnerved her. She nearly ran up the walk to the front door. The receptionist buzzed her in. She signed in then strode down to LJ's room.

"Mama!" LJ's face split into a wide grin as he spotted his mother when she entered his classroom.

She wanted to wilt against the wall. He was safe. No one had hurt him. Had she overreacted? No. She couldn't take a chance.

LJ's teacher, Miss Prince, sat at a large kidney-shaped table, reading with a student.

"I'll be right back, Zoe." She stood and walked over to Jennie. "Hi, Jennie. I didn't know you were coming now."

"I'm taking LJ home early." Jennie rubbed a shaking hand through her boy's curls. "Get your backpack, buddy. We're leaving."

"Goody!" He hugged her. "Are we going home, Mama?"

Jennie didn't answer. It didn't matter. He was already gone, to get his belongings, chattering to his friends that he was leaving early.

"Will you be back tomorrow?" Miss Prince smiled at him as he stopped again next to Jennie. "It's the last day before we're off."

Jennie startled. "Oh. I forgot. Next week is Christmas break."

"That's right." Miss Prince nodded. "With Christmas on Thursday, the schools around here are closed all next week. He'll have school off until January 2."

Fourteen days before she'd need to decide what to do. The relief washed over her. She didn't need to worry about making up an excuse as to why LJ wouldn't be back. Because there was no way she was sending him to school until the danger was past.

What if it never was? Would she ever be free of the past?

Once in the parking lot, she glanced around, searching for anything suspicious.

"Look, Mama! Santa!"

Turning her head, she saw the man she'd passed earlier climbing onto a motorcycle. He looked ridiculous. Without a glance her way, he rumbled down the street and around the corner. She felt silly, letting him bother her. Regardless, she stumbled to the driver's door in her haste to get out of the parking lot.

At home, she looked all the way around her car before turning it off. Not seeing anything, she quickly exited the vehicle and then moved around to the back to get her son. She kept a tight hold on his hand as they entered the building.

Her phone rang. She grimaced. It was Randi again. She placed the earbuds in her ears as they arrived at the apartment.

She forgot about answering the call when she twisted the knob and remembered with dismay that she had left the door unlocked in her haste. Unease rocked in her belly.

She opened the door with caution and peeked in before entering.

Nothing was out of place. The apartment looked just as she'd left it when she'd rushed out. Moving inside, she heard glass breaking under her foot as she stepped on an ornament.

Alarm shivered up her spine. The ornaments had landed on the tree skirt, not on her carpet. With a shriek, she spun full circle, coming face-to-face with Santa Claus. It was the man she'd seen on the street.

He was too large to be Steve.

He launched himself at her, grabbing the earbud cord hooked to her phone. He quickly wrapped it around her throat and pulled. She couldn't breathe!

LJ screamed and launched himself at the man. The stranger shoved him away with a casual swipe before focusing again on Jennie.

She was going to die. What would happen to her son?

A moment later the cord around her neck went limp and the Santa was pulled away by two Amish men rushing through the open door. The Santa bounced off the wall with a vicious yell, his white beard lying on the floor of the apartment. She'd never seen him before in her life. Her eyes rose to meet his briefly. A shiver ran through her at his cold glare. He tore his gaze away before turning and bolting from the apartment. His heavy footsteps thundered down the stairs.

She was too shocked to care. Her world shrank down to the man standing in front of her, staring at her with confused eyes. Eyes she saw every day when she looked at their son.

Luke, the man she'd mourned for nearly five years, was standing in front of her, looking at her like she was a complete stranger.

TWO

"Luke." She was dazed, confused.

It was Luke, wasn't it? His face was altered. A long, jagged scar ran the length of his right cheek. His left profile, though, was the same as she remembered. His hair was longer than he'd worn it while they were married. It was still blond and curly but was in the typical bowl-cut style she'd seen on the Amish men in the surrounding area.

A chill swept through her. What had happened to him? How was it that the man she'd loved and mourned was standing before her dressed like an Amish man? He'd left that life behind when they got married.

"Mama, Mama." LJ ran to her side, clinging to her legs. Her sweet baby. She squatted down to peer into his eyes. He seemed uninjured. Terrified, but other than that, unharmed. She stood and lifted him in her arms, settling his weight against her hip. LJ rested his head on her shoulder. She dropped a kiss on his curls.

When she glanced up, she saw that both men were watching her. Luke's eyes were still puzzled. Disappointment sizzled through her at the lack of tenderness he displayed. Had he used the accident to return to his community? They had never even discussed the possibility of her becoming Amish. She'd thought he was happy with their life.

Raymond's gaze, however, was much more concerned. Actually, as he focused his attention on her son, dread was dawning in his gaze.

He doesn't know, she realized. Raymond had no idea that she and Luke had been a couple. Was her husband ashamed of her?

She opened her mouth to say something. Then closed it. She didn't even know where to begin.

"I think we need to decide what to do about the man who attacked you before we get sidetracked by anything else." Raymond laid a hand on Luke's shoulder all the while staring at Jennie and LJ. His voice interrupted her musings. She put her questions aside for the moment. He was right.

Luke rubbed his chin, his eyes never leaving her face. He still looked perplexed. "I saw a news report this morning. A man named Steve Curtis escaped from prison. I don't know why, but I thought you might be in danger."

Luke's voice was the same one she remembered, softly spoken and deep, with just the barest edge of gravel in it. *Textured*—that was the word that came to mind when she thought of his voice. His words struck her as odd. "You don't know?"

He'd rescued her from Steve once before. That was how they had met. After that, she'd worked with Luke for several years on various housing projects. They'd been inseparable, and she had shared everything about her past with him. Surely, he had to know that the man was a menace.

Luke opened his mouth. "How do—"

"Later." Raymond narrowed his gaze at his brother. Jennie itched to ask Luke what he was about to say. "He got away. Now what?"

She shook her head. They'd both seen her attacker's face. She didn't understand the confusion. "That was not Steve Curtis."

"Are you sure?" Doubt rang clear in Raymond's voice.

"Of course," she bit out. Then winced at the curt tone. Well, she had both their attention now. "I don't know who it was. He didn't speak, although I think his intent was clear." She rubbed her throat with the hand that wasn't holding on to her son. "I guess we should call the police."

She didn't give either man the chance to argue, not that either of them made a sound as she pulled out her phone and dialed. While they waited, she went into the kitchen under the guise of getting her son something to eat. In truth, she wasn't sure if she was more unsettled by the escape of her stepfather and her subsequent attack, or the reappearance of her deceased spouse.

Within fifteen minutes, two Pennsylvania State Police troopers stood inside her apartment. Raymond and Luke discreetly edged toward the kitchen, letting her talk with the troopers privately.

"We'll want to talk with you, too, when we're done," one of the troopers said to Luke and Raymond.

Luke frowned, but neither he nor his brother protested. Jennie remembered that the Amish she'd met while she and Luke had been together hadn't been keen about involving outside law enforcement, for anything.

The troopers efficiently took her statement, then

went about investigating the apartment. One trooper headed out into the hall and the other disappeared into the kitchen.

"You said you saw this man at your son's preschool?" the trooper in the hall asked.

She nodded. "Yeah. I saw him leaving the school on a motorcycle as we were walking to the car. He must have taken a shortcut."

"Did you see the motorcycle when you arrived home?"

She resisted the urge to roll her eyes. "No. If I'd seen it, I wouldn't have gotten out of my car."

He accepted that with a grunt and made a note on his tablet. Her mind wandered.

Her attacker had been inside waiting for her. Just the idea of someone hiding in the home that she shared with her son made her queasy. He must have beaten her there by mere seconds. Where had he parked the motorcycle? She knew she hadn't seen it. He must have parked in the back of the building and come in through that entrance.

She frowned. Who was he? It had to have been Steve's doing. No one else had anything against her. Steve, however, had gone to prison not once, but twice, because of her. The second time, she was sure he'd be there until he died.

How had he escaped prison?

And almost as important—who had helped him?

What if Steve came next to finish up his lackey's failed attempt? The questions continued to whirl through her brain like a vortex, making her dizzy.

Suddenly the haven she lived in seemed like a cage.

They couldn't stay there. But where could they go? A longing for her brother welled up inside her. Aiden would know what to do. Not only was he her older brother, but he used to be a cop before he married Sophie and began teaching criminal justice at a university. But he wasn't even in the country. He didn't plan to return until next week. She had no family other than Aiden. She didn't have enough money saved up for a hotel, nor would she feel comfortable in such a place.

And what about her job? She dismissed that as unimportant. She could always find another job. Companies were always looking for tech support. And she knew that she was skilled with computers and other technology.

Panic was pulsing in her veins when the first trooper tromped back up the steps and into the apartment. In his hands, he held a cheap Santa suit.

"Fresh motorcycle tracks in the yard out back near the dumpster," he reported.

She'd been right. Not that it brought any comfort.

Within half an hour, the troopers were ready to leave. As it was a few minutes shy of noon, most of the other tenants were at work. Their parking lot had no camera surveillance, so even if her attacker had parked in the lot outside, there was no record of it. Jennie had never taken note of what kinds of vehicles were parked at the apartment complex on a daily basis.

The troopers quietly talked with Luke and Raymond for a few minutes before returning to ask Jennie to come down to the station later to look at some images in their data files.

"You got a look at his face," one trooper remarked. "It's possible that you might be able to ID him."

"Of course." She didn't want to, but it wasn't like she had a choice.

"Thanks." The trooper smiled and walked out the door. "Come in soon, Mrs. Beiler." The door shut behind him and his partner.

"What?" the brothers said simultaneously.

Shocked, Jennie turned to stare at them.

"Your last name was Forster," Raymond insisted.

Luke's face was the color of all-purpose flour. "Why did they call you Mrs. Beiler?"

Astonishment held her frozen as the truth finally sank in. He didn't remember her. Jennie swallowed hard.

"Because that's who I am." She narrowed her eyes at him, took in the disbelief, the shock as he swayed on his feet before catching himself. "We were married six years ago. This is your son. And I am your wife."

His wife. He had a wife. And a son?

His shattered heart started beating like a freight train. Was that sweet little boy with the blond hair and blue eyes truly his flesh and blood? But why would this woman lie? This woman that seemed so familiar, yet not. It seemed incredible that he could have forgotten this lovely woman with her dark brown hair, hanging in a ponytail partway down her back. Her eyes were dark brown with glimmers of gold in them. There was such an air of fragility about her, but he could also sense that she had a solid core of strength.

"I—I was in an accident. I have no memories of my life from seventeen until I was twenty-two." He forced the words out of his tight throat. How did someone forget that they have a wife? "How old is your son?"

He winced at her frown. He couldn't say *our son*. It just wasn't real to him. Not yet.

"Here," Raymond interrupted. "Let me take him, *jah*? We will go into the other room while you two talk."

The child wasn't keen on the idea of leaving his mother at first, but Raymond managed to coax him out of her arms. As soon as Luke was alone with Jennie, he moved over to sit on the couch. She joined him but sat perched on the edge, ready to take flight at a moment's notice.

Had they had a good marriage? At least he knew why she had seemed so familiar to him even though he was missing a huge chunk of his memories.

"To get back to your question about our son—" he didn't miss the emphasis on the word *our* "—he's four. I had just found out I was pregnant when they told me you were dead. I was devastated." Her lovely brown eyes glistened with tears. "The baby was all I had left. LJ is my whole world."

"LJ?"

"Luke Junior." She shook her head. "I was told you were killed in an explosion at the plant you worked at. I buried an empty casket because there was no body. If only I had known you were still alive!"

She huffed and hugged her arms across her stomach. For a scant second, anger blazed out of her eyes. Then her lovely face changed, became sad.

He felt that sadness all the way to his bones. "I had no idea who I was. I woke up in a ditch, my leg injured and clothes in tatters. In fact, I thought I was still seventeen."

Her eyes grew huge and her mouth dropped open.

He nodded in understanding. "When I returned home to *Mamm* and *Daed*, they told me that I was twenty-two and had been gone for several years. I couldn't recall any of it."

"Until today?"

His heart broke at the hope in her voice. He shook his head, shattering that hope. "*Nee*, I still have no memory. Not really. When I saw that news report, I knew that man was no *gut*. In my mind, I could see your face, but I had no idea why."

She sighed.

"Jennie, can you tell me about Steve Curtis? When I saw his picture, all I could think was that you were in danger. I didn't remember who you were, but I did know that you were important."

For the briefest moment, her eyes softened. It was gone so fast he might have imagined it.

"I hate talking about him."

Luke waited. He couldn't force her to tell him, but he hoped she would.

She sighed. "Fine. I've already told the police everything. I guess it won't hurt to repeat it one more time." Slapping her hands down on her knees, she pushed herself to a stand. Then she removed her hair from the band that was holding it loosely at the back of her neck. He was momentarily distracted by the wealth of shining brown hair streaming down her back before she caught it up again in a tighter ponytail.

"When I was a kid, my mother married Steve. My brother, Aiden, and I didn't know at first how terrible he was. But soon we found out. While Mom was at work, Steve was at home, drunk and angry. He attacked me when I was eleven."

Luke froze, horrified.

"My brother went after him and knocked him down,

then locked us in my bedroom. The police arrested Steve and he stood trial. I had to testify. It was awful. His defense attorney tore me apart. Somehow, it was my fault. I was a kid. The jury didn't buy it, and he was sentenced to four years in prison. Four years!" She snorted.

Luke couldn't speak. He clenched his fists to hold in the anger rushing through him.

She wasn't done. "My brother and I thought we were free, but we weren't. We were taken away from my mom and placed in foster care. In separate homes. My mom had had enough and gave us up. I blamed Aiden for years for not protecting me. For leaving me. But he was only fifteen. When he aged out of the foster care system, he came to find me, but I wanted nothing to do with him. We didn't actually reconcile until almost five years ago."

"What about your mom?"

She shrugged. "I never saw her again."

"Steve, he was released four years later?"

"Yeah." Her voice crackled, as if her throat were suddenly dry. She cleared it. "Actually, it was less than four years. And he came after me, to pay me back for costing him everything. I was fifteen. You were on your *rumspringa*. I was walking back to my current foster home after school, and suddenly he was there with a knife." She rubbed her shoulder. "You heard me scream and rushed to my rescue. He assaulted me, but you were in time to save my life."

She'd had to be strong to survive the blows life had dealt her and still be able to love and nurture a child. And apparently, she'd once loved Luke, too. Now he understood the strength he'd sensed about her.

He swallowed. He could clearly see the scene in his

mind, the stabbing knife, the blood on her shoulder. And he knew the knife wound hadn't been the worst part of the attack. His heart ached for her.

"When I was released from the hospital," she went on, "my foster parents decided that it was too dangerous to bring me back into their home."

He blinked. "You hadn't done anything wrong."

"I had someone coming after me. Even though Steve would go to jail, they didn't want me. I ended up in a new foster home, close to your uncle's house."

"You worked on housing projects with us, building homes, didn't you?"

She smiled, just the smallest lift of the corners of her mouth. He found himself wanting to see a full smile from her. "I did. I was relegated to do the painting. Your uncle said I was hopeless with a hammer. Kept dropping all the nails."

Luke wanted to find out more. There were still so many questions that weren't answered.

"Do you—" She stopped.

He waited, frustrated when she didn't continue. "Do I what?"

She grabbed a hank of hair lying over her right shoulder and began to twist it around her fingers. He remembered that gesture. It meant she was unsure of herself. He wanted to tell her she could ask him anything, but held his tongue, not wanting to make her more flustered than she already was.

"I was just wondering… Well, I know you lost some of your memories."

More like five years' worth of memories. His gaze zeroed in on the pictures on the wall. Pictures of LJ as a baby until now. His son's entire life. He nodded for her to continue.

"Well, do you, you know, still have nightmares about fires?"

His mouth dropped open. He closed it. His teeth clicked. Swiping his hand across his top lip, he wiped away the sweat that had formed at the mere thought of being trapped inside a blazing building. "*Jah*, I do. Did I tell you about the fire?"

She nodded. "Not everything—you were kinda closemouthed about it. But I know that you were in a fire when you were fourteen and one of your cousins died."

His cousin had died because Luke had failed to pull him out of the inferno. It wasn't something he was willing to talk about. Maybe one day, but not yet. Especially not with a woman who was a virtual stranger to him, no matter how they might have been connected.

Raymond exited the kitchen with LJ. LJ's face had a smear of jelly in the corner of his mouth. "He said he was hungry, so I made him a peanut-butter-and-jelly sandwich."

"That's fine," Jennie said.

"I know you guys have a lot to talk about, but are you going to the police station soon?"

"I should go now."

"I'm coming with you," Luke blurted out. When they both stared at him, he grew irritated. "What?"

"What do I tell the driver?" Raymond demanded. "Or what do I tell *Mamm* and *Daed*?"

Luke stared at his brother. Why was any of that important? He had just found out he had a wife and child. It seemed obvious that everything else would be a lower priority right now. He cut his eyes to Jennie. She hadn't responded. He tilted his head to the side and lifted his eyebrows at her, a silent question.

"Nothing," Jennie mumbled.

He was disappointed. Her voice gave no indication of how she felt about him now. Not that he had any idea what his own feelings were. They were a jumbled mess. However, the truth was that he had a wife and a son, even if he didn't know them. He wasn't leaving her alone again.

"Mama," LJ said, tugging at Jennie's jeans.

"Yes, pumpkin?"

"Who is that?" LJ pointed a timid finger at Luke.

There was a pause. "That, LJ, is your daddy."

"I have a daddy?" LJ beamed a wide grin across the room at Luke.

Luke blinked as his vision blurred.

Nee, he was not leaving. Not now.

THREE

"This is not a *gut* idea," Raymond hissed at Luke the moment Jennie had taken LJ into the bathroom to help the child wash his face and brush his teeth. "You should come home with me."

"I can't leave yet. You know I can't. Not when I know I have a wife and son."

"A wife who is not Plain."

Luke rubbed his chest against the ache that was already forming there. Jennie was a stranger to him, true. But she was his wife. Even if they could never be together, either because they were strangers, or because he was now part of the Amish church. It was an impossible situation. "*Jah*, I know she is not Plain."

"Then why—"

Luke rounded on his brother. "Would you have me abandon her, abandon my *son*, when they are in danger?" His voice had dropped to a growl. He knew his brother meant well, but he was not leaving Jennie to deal with this crisis on her own. "What if you were in my position and discovered you and Mary Ellen were married and had a child? Would you abandon her? Could you?"

Raymond struggled with it for a moment longer before finally giving in. "I wouldn't. You're right. How will you get home?"

Luke understood the underlying question. Raymond wanted his assurance that he would return home. He wasn't ready to give that. Not yet. Finding he had a family had unsettled him. He couldn't abandon them, even if Jennie was unwilling to trust him. He couldn't blame her for being that way, but still, he was determined to stay close. He would protect them as well as he could.

"I'll manage when it's time."

That was no answer. But it was the best he could do.

Jennie and LJ walked out of the bathroom. The boy was chattering happily to his mother about how cool the troopers had been. He'd obviously gotten over the fact that someone had been inside the apartment.

Luke could hardly force his eyes away from the boy. A surge of emotion swept over him, closing his throat. He'd missed four years of this boy's life. If he and Raymond hadn't shown up today, both Jennie and LJ might now be dead.

He shook off the morose thought. He couldn't allow himself to dwell on it.

"I'm heading back home, Jennie." Raymond shoved his hat back on his head and shrugged back into his winter coat.

Jennie raised her eyebrows at him.

"I'm staying." Luke caught the look she cast his way. Jennie was not one to tolerate someone telling her what to do. "If that's okay? Please?"

She looked like she wanted to argue.

LJ latched onto his hand. "Yay! Daddy's going to stay, Mama!"

He fought back the rush of emotion that threatened to overwhelm him. His son wanted him to stay. He'd never missed having his memory more than he did at this bittersweet moment. If he'd remembered who he was, maybe he wouldn't have missed his son's first four years. He lifted his gaze to Jennie, silently begging her to allow him this time.

Her mouth tightened. But she just gave a weary nod. "Fine."

The tension left his shoulders. He followed her out to her car so they could go to the police station. She fastened LJ into his booster chair in the back while Luke settled himself in the passenger seat. At one point, he must have known how to drive a car, he mused. He'd probably done it on a daily basis. He had no recollection of it and wasn't even sure he'd be able to figure it out without embarrassing himself. It didn't matter. He was content to ride along.

Raymond climbed up into the van beside Sam. The brothers shared one last glance. Raymond's gaze warned him to take care. Luke kept his face blank. Finally, Raymond and Sam pulled out and drove away.

Jennie got into the driver's side and fastened her seat belt.

"Thanks for letting me stay." Luke kept his voice low, hyperaware of the child a few feet away from him.

Jennie didn't answer at first, focusing on backing out of her space. "I still can't believe you're alive." Her voice was thick with too many emotions for him to decipher them all.

"I'm sure it's a shock. I wish I'd remembered sooner." That was putting it mildly.

She bit her lip. She flipped on the radio, probably

to mask their voices. "Luke, I don't know what we're supposed to do in this situation. I was told you were dead. I went through the pregnancy alone, always feeling like I was in a bad dream, but that one day you'd walk through the door. But after LJ was born, I had to accept that you were gone. I had him to focus on, and it helped. But raising a child on my own wasn't easy."

He was sure it wasn't. And now that LJ was four, she no doubt didn't appreciate Luke's reappearance, complicating her life. Even if he had just saved it.

"I remembered this apartment," he commented, waving his hand toward the building as they drove away from it. "I don't know how, but when we were driving here, I was able to lead the driver straight here." He paused a moment. "I would have thought you'd have moved."

After she heard he'd died, but he didn't add that part. She seemed to understand.

"I told the landlord that I wouldn't be renewing my lease in February. My brother and his wife, Sophie, have a place near Pittsburgh. Sophie's sister is deaf and attends the residential school there as a day student. I decided to move closer to them."

He never would have found them if she had already moved. He forced his mind away from that thought. It wasn't productive to think of what might have happened.

"Are you upset to find that I'm alive?" he asked instead.

"Oh!" Her eyes flared open wide at his question. "Of course not! It's good that you survived the explosion. Of course it is. It's just…"

He waited, his heart pounding. He wasn't sure he wanted to know what she was trying to say.

"Just what?" he prompted when she looked as if she wasn't going to continue.

She was pulling into the police station. She shifted in her seat and met his gaze head-on. "I don't know you anymore. Which must sound selfish of me. I'm sorry, truly I am. I know that you've lost your memories. I can't even imagine how that must feel."

"It's disconcerting, that's for sure. There's a gap in my mind, a large chunk of experiences that I don't recall. Things that I might have learned how to do that I can't do anymore." Should he say it? "It's also painful to know that I've been a father for four years and have missed it."

"I understand that." Her voice was soft. He had to strain to catch her words. "I'm just not certain how to proceed. You're a stranger to me. And my life has finally gotten to a point where I feel like I'm moving forward. Or it was."

What had changed that more, knowing he was alive or knowing that Steve was out to get her? Steve. What were they doing sitting in a car when that man was still out there, waiting for the opportunity to attack again?

"We need to get inside. We're vulnerable here." He wished they had more time, but the situation was urgent.

She opened her door, and he followed her example. They gathered up LJ and headed into the station. Would he open up to him again? The frustration was gnawing at him. If only he could remember.

"We need to talk more." He broke the silence that had settled between them.

"I know. But not now."

LJ was trotting along beside his mother, his hand in hers, when he reached out and grabbed Luke's left hand in his free hand. Luke smiled down at his son, still in awe that he had a child.

Jennie signed in at the reception desk. The clerk who was behind a glass window buzzed them into the station.

Luke was aware of eyes following them as they walked into the room. It probably wasn't every day that an Amish man showed up in their station with an *Englisch* woman.

They didn't have to wait long before they were met by one of the troopers that had been out to the apartment earlier. Carter, his badge said. He led them back into a separate room, away from everyone else. Luke was glad to be away from the curious stares.

"Okay, Jennie. Luke. There's no rush. Take your time and look through the images. I'll stay here. Let me know if you recognize anyone."

Within a few minutes, Jennie and Luke were seated at a console, looking at images of possible suspects. It was chilling to realize how many images they would need to look through. Luke felt hemmed in behind the console. He wasn't used to being surrounded by so much technology.

Or maybe it was the fact that he was sitting in an *Englisch* police station that made him feel like ants were crawling under his skin.

A woman walked in and tried to convince LJ to go with her, but the child pressed against his mother and refused to budge.

"Not going." He turned his face into Jennie's side.

"I'd like him to stay with me," Jennie said, hugging her son.

"It's okay, Anne. He can stay with us," Trooper Carter told her.

Luke was relieved when the woman gave in. He didn't want to let the boy out of his sight, either, although he was probably safe at the police station.

"Hey, Mama!" LJ yelled out five minutes later, pointing at the screen. "I seen that man before."

Carter moved quickly. He eyed the man on the screen, then turned his sharp gaze to LJ. "Are you sure, son? You've seen this man?"

LJ nodded. "He stands outside the playground taking pictures of me and my friends."

Jennie's hands froze as the blood drained from her face. Luke wanted to bolt out the door and find the man immediately. He forced himself to remain still. Someone was watching his son. Was Steve behind this, or were more people out to destroy his family?

Jennie wanted to grab up her son and run. Where, she had no idea.

Someone was watching her baby. She didn't think she could handle any more shocks. Having Luke appear this morning had been hard, but this was worse. Much worse. She had to keep her mind from exploring the many possible scenarios that could have happened before she realized they were in danger.

LJ is fine. They'd protect him.

Trooper Carter immediately left the room after noting the name of the man who'd been watching the playground.

"This can't be a coincidence." Luke's face was like granite.

Funny, she'd not noticed that hardness in him before. Luke had always been so gentle and easygoing. Not now. The man beside her was intense. The look in his eyes as he gazed at LJ told her more than words could that he was taking his new fatherhood seriously.

Her pulse stuttered. What did it mean for them that he was back? They were married, but she didn't know if that mattered anymore. He was obviously Amish again. She was not.

Not to mention the fact that she didn't know him anymore.

Trooper Carter returned. "The school has been informed that a known felon has been spotted around their premises. Oliver Deets is his name. He's been busted on some petty crimes. A car has been sent out to his last known residence to bring him in for questioning."

Carter inquired if they needed anything more before leaving them again. Jennie continued looking though the images, but her mind was on the alert, willing someone to come and give them more information. It was hard to focus when her mind kept replaying the moment when LJ had said someone had been taking pictures of him at school. How much more could they take? It seemed unreal that a full-grown man could stalk preschool children and no one would notice.

Finally, she backed away from the database. Carter returned. "Have you finished?" he asked.

"Yes. I didn't see the man who attacked me in there."

"Okay. I'm going to take you to the conference room to wait until we have more information."

It was a tense group that waited for the next hour in

the conference room. Luke tended to pace. She remembered that habit from when they were together. Jennie kept to her seat, but only because LJ was sitting so close to her. The child seemed to sense something was wrong.

When the door opened again and Carter appeared with a younger trooper, the flat expression on his face chilled her blood.

"We didn't find Deets in his apartment. It was obvious that he'd fled. We did, however, find these."

He handed her a couple photographs of the walls in Deets's apartment. One wall had been filled with pictures that Deets had obviously taken. Bile rose in her throat as she looked at dozens of candid shots. LJ at school. She and LJ at the store. Getting into her car to leave in the morning. The pictures spanned back two months. For two months, this man had been trailing her and her son, documenting their every move outside the apartment.

There was even a picture of an article relating to her brother's wedding. Were Aiden and his family in jeopardy?

She pointed a shaking finger at the article. "That's my brother's wedding, several years back. Aiden, that's my brother—he used to be a cop—he's out of the country right now."

Trooper Carter nodded. "We'll be notifying him of the possible dangers. I'm sure he'll know what to do."

That was true. A small part of her relaxed at that. But not much. There didn't seem to be a part of their life the stalker had missed.

This was not a spur-of-the moment attack. This was a planned-out offensive. But how? How had Steve orchestrated this from prison? What else did he have up his sleeve that she wasn't aware of?

"What should we do?" Luke asked, his voice low. Jennie blinked at him. It might have been her imagination, but his voice almost sounded dangerous. Which seemed odd when combined with his Amish attire.

But he'd lived away from the Amish for several years. He might not remember those years, but could those experiences be affecting his responses anyway?

Trooper Carter met his gaze. "Don't play the hero. If you see anything, let us know. We'll be watching for any movement around the apartment. Keep your doors locked. I would suggest not going out alone."

She understood. Trooper Carter wanted them to stay together. She was relieved. As much as Luke's reappearance had unsettled her, she was glad she wouldn't be on her own.

"We could put you up in a hotel," Trooper Carter said.

She was shaking her head before he finished speaking. At Steve's trial, it had become apparent that she was not his only victim over the years. However, he had many friends and connections. She wasn't going to go anywhere that a stranger might have access to. At least her landlord was familiar. She knew he was a Christian man.

Jennie hadn't wanted anything to do with God since she'd landed in the foster care system. In her mind, He'd turned his back on her and failed to protect her when she needed Him most. She still respected that others had faith. And she knew enough of the landlord to believe that he would not be in league with criminals.

There weren't many others she could be sure of.

"LJ won't be returning to preschool," she decided out loud. If he did, it would not be to the same school. She could never drop him off again without recalling that a man had been scoping out the school. That trust had been broken.

"That's probably for the best, at least until we have more information." Trooper Carter gathered up the pictures again. She was happy to have them out of her hands.

It was after four by the time they finally left the station. The temperature had dropped, and it had started to snow while they were inside. Soft, fluffy white flakes that looked like they belonged in a snow globe dusted the landscape. The beauty of it was at odds with the ugliness of what was happening inside her world.

"We're out of milk," she said.

"Excuse me?" Luke replied.

Jennie blushed. "Sorry. This morning, I went shopping, but I dropped the milk when I found out Steve was out of prison. I need to stop by the store."

He nodded, a slight smile curling the corners of his mouth. "Then let's stop and get some."

She suddenly realized that Luke was going to be coming home with her and LJ. She couldn't get over the fact that he hadn't been killed.

She cast a sidelong glance at him. He hadn't said anything since they'd exited the building. His face was mostly closed off, but even as she watched, a grimace of pain crossed his brow.

He was limping.

"Did you hurt your leg when you pulled that man off me?"

He looked at her, brow creased in puzzlement.

"You're limping. I thought you might have been hurt."

"*Jah*, I know I have a slight limp. I told you I injured my leg. It was a partial fracture, but it still pains me at times."

"Sorry. Didn't mean to pry." A flush stole up her cheeks. She hoped he didn't think she was rude for pointing it out.

He shrugged. "*Nee*, don't be sorry. I'm used to it now. I get by."

She nodded. Without comment, they bundled LJ into the car. She was so weary, but LJ always wanted milk with his dinner. The drive to the store was silent. Jennie couldn't get up the energy to talk. It seemed no one else wanted to, either. Every few seconds, she heard a small murmur from her son. With each sound, she tensed a little more. LJ being quiet was not a good thing. It usually meant he was upset or sick.

They pulled into the grocery store parking lot three minutes later. Jennie found a space near the middle and pulled in. Her car was boxed in by a truck in front of her and an SUV on either side. She turned off the engine, leaned her head back against the seat and closed her eyes. Just for a moment.

"Jennie? Are you all right?" Luke asked.

She sighed. No, she wasn't all right. "I'm fine. Let's do this and go home."

Mentally bracing herself, she pushed open the door and got out, stretching for just a moment before she opened the back door to get LJ. She contemplated asking Luke to wait in the car with him, but quickly decided against it. The idea of letting LJ out of her sight for five minutes made her stomach clench.

She stretched her mouth into what she hoped was a cheerful smile. "Come on, LJ. We're on a mission to score some milk."

Normally, her son loved "going on missions." Today was not one of those days. He scrunched up his little face in a scowl.

"I'm tired," LJ said. Oh, no. She knew that voice. Her son was getting close to an exhaustion-driven melt down. She needed to get into the store and get the milk before that happened.

"Hey, LJ, want me to carry you?" Luke appeared at her side.

The boy's eyes lit up at his father's question. "Yeah!"

Jennie moved away to let Luke get LJ out of his seat. When she heard her son laugh, she turned away to hide the sudden tears in her eyes. She'd often thought about how much Luke would have loved being a father. She walked to the back of her car to wait for them, hoping the space would allow her to get her balance back.

A sharp squeal of tires rent the air. A car turned the corner of the parking lot and was racing down the aisle.

It was going to hit her. Jennie's legs wouldn't move. Had Steve come to take her out at last?

FOUR

The car was almost to her when she felt two strong arms wrap around her waist. Luke pulled her out of the main lane and threw her against the driver's door of her car, slamming the back door shut at the same time. He flattened himself against her back, shielding her from danger with his own body. They were guarded on either side by the SUVs parked there.

The driver swerved away, nicking the bumper of her car, before barreling out of the parking lot. If only she could see his face! Was it Oliver Deets, the man who'd been watching her son?

Tires squealed as the vehicle roared off down the street.

Jennie's heart was pounding inside her chest so hard it was painful. "LJ!" she managed to gasp out.

Luke stepped away from her and opened the back door. LJ was still sitting in his booster seat, his eyes wide and confused. The buckle was undone.

A chill went down her spine. Five seconds later, and Luke and LJ might have been out there in the parking lot with her.

"Thanks," she murmured to Luke, her blood still roaring in her ears. "That was a close one."

Luke stared at her, his eyes narrowed as they scanned her face. "Are you hurt? I threw you against the car pretty hard."

"No. Terrified at what almost happened, yes. And definitely grateful that you acted so quickly. But not hurt."

"Did you get a look at the man who was driving the car?"

She heard what he didn't ask. Was it Steve? She shook her head, frustrated. "No! I was too panicked. And the sun was in my eyes, so I couldn't see anything." A new thought struck her. "Did we get a look at the car? And by we, I mainly mean you, because I only know that it was blue."

He shrugged. "It was blue, four doors. Looked like your average small sedan."

"So, no." She used to tease him that he was the only guy she knew who wasn't into cars. Growing up Amish, cars weren't something he paid attention to.

He looked at her for another second. "Do we abandon the milk run?"

She was so tempted to say yes. But then she looked at LJ. "No, let's go get milk and then go home. LJ won't understand if we don't get it."

How did you explain all that was happening to a four-year-old?

Luke hefted LJ in his arms, pretending the child weighed a ton to make him laugh, and then they power walked into the store, both of them constantly scanning the now peaceful parking lot. In the store, she grabbed two gallons, because she remembered Luke liked milk, too. Then she pushed past the lines with cashiers and went to the self check-out area. She normally avoided those. After dealing with technology all day on the job, it was nice to have some human interaction. But today she wanted to be done and home, locked in her own space.

They were back in her car in under ten minutes and on their way to her apartment. When they pulled in, she realized that home no longer provided the safe feeling she'd had before she left for the store earlier that morning.

"You know," she commented in a low voice to Luke, "when I woke up this morning, everything was normal. Now I have people trying to kill me, my home has been invaded and my husband has returned from the dead with no memory. I think that sets a record for weird days."

He didn't answer for a moment. "I don't know what to say to that. I'm sorry that I left you alone, although it wasn't something I planned."

She opened her mouth, ready to protest that she hadn't meant for him to feel bad, but he raised a hand. She shut her mouth to listen.

"I don't remember the time we spent together, but I am getting flashes. Insights? Maybe memories of feelings rather than actual events? I'm not sure. Maybe I'll remember more, maybe not. But I do want you to know that I never would have left you alone intentionally."

"I know that, Luke. That wasn't the type of person you were. You weren't a great one for planning, but you were never negligent. You were always responsible." She cleared her throat. "Let's go in, get out of the open."

Anything to change the subject.

When they arrived at her apartment door, she paused again, uneasy. "The last time I came home, someone had invaded it."

Luke gently nudged her aside. She stepped back, LJ at her side, while he checked the lock. When it wouldn't budge, he held out his hand. "Key," he mouthed. She nodded and dropped the key into his waiting palm. Briefly, the pads of her fingers tapped his palm. The warmth singeing them was familiar. She ignored it. Now was not the time.

He slowly unlocked the door, trying to be as quiet as possible. They entered the living room together. Luke held a finger to his lips and pointed to the wall next to the door. Jennie nodded in understanding, then moved herself and LJ so that they were both standing with their backs against the wall.

She watched, her gut aching with anxiety, as Luke walked with whisper-soft steps to the kitchen. He exited a few moments later, then disappeared down the hall. She strained her ears and heard the bathroom door open. The bedroom doors were already open wide.

LJ started to speak. Quickly she shushed him, then squatted down to his level.

"We have to be quiet until Daddy comes back," she whispered to her son.

"Is Daddy on a mission, Mama?"

"Um, yeah, you could say that."

"If he finishes his mission, can we have ice cream?" His blue eyes were hopeful.

Her heart melted, even while she wanted to cry. Her son was so innocent; he had no idea of the evil that had entered his world. She wanted to keep him ignorant of it as long as she could, if it was possible.

She was also impressed with his burgeoning barter-ing skills. "If you don't talk until he returns, then yes."

His sparkling eyes told her he wouldn't say a word until Luke returned.

Twenty seconds later, Luke walked back into the room, his smile and nod letting her know all was clear. Only then did the knot in her belly melt. She let out the breath she'd been holding in a long whoosh.

LJ tugged at her arm. When she looked down at him, he pointed at Luke, then he jabbed his finger at his mouth. Jennie let out a laugh, her first real laugh all day.

Luke raised his eyebrows. "What'd I miss?"

She bent to kiss the top of LJ's curly hair. "Your son was very good and quiet while you were on your mis-sion to check out the apartment. He gets ice cream as a reward."

Luke's eyes went soft at the words *your son*. She fussed with LJ's hair a moment longer, pretending not to notice until she heard Luke clear his throat.

"Chocolate chip cookie dough?" he asked. His eyes lit up, reminding her of LJ.

She snorted. "What do you think? Is there any other kind?"

"Yay!" LJ raced to the kitchen. She could hear him climbing into his booster seat at the table.

She and Luke followed after him, both of them more relaxed than they had been five minutes earlier.

She scooped out the ice cream into three bowls.

"The hard stuff, Mama."

She reached into the cupboard and grabbed the homemade chocolate shell topping. She shook it up and poured a generous amount on LJ's ice cream. He tapped it with his spoon.

"Give it a few more seconds, honey. It needs some time to harden."

When he tapped again, his spoon thunked against the hard coating. "Oh, goody. It's ready!"

"Hey, I want to try some, too." Luke held out his bowl. Jennie rolled her eyes, but complied and poured the chocolate goodness on his treat. Then she shrugged and added some to her own bowl. She usually tried to watch what she ate, but she deserved something special after the day she'd had.

Luke and LJ both bit into their ice cream. LJ looked at his father. "Yum!"

"*Jah*, it is yum."

Jennie snickered but refrained from commenting. A few minutes later, she collected the bowls and washed them. LJ took Luke to show him his room and his toys. Jennie looked at her phone. The light was blinking. She pushed Play to listen to the message.

"Jennie, it's Randi. Hey, when you get this message, call me, please? It's important."

She frowned. When she'd talked with Randi earlier that day, Randi had been her normal chatty self. Her voice on the answering machine sounded tense.

Jennie picked up her phone and called Randi. It rang four times before going to voice mail. "It's me, Jennie. I'll be available all evening. Call me back."

She hung up, still frowning, wondering what Randi could have wanted. A voice in her mind whispered that maybe it had something to do with Steve, but that was ridiculous. Randi had never even met Steve. And what she did know about him from Jennie was vague. The only person Jennie had ever shared everything with was Luke.

Not even Aiden knew everything. He knew that Steve had attacked her when she was eleven, but she'd never told him that their stepfather had raped her when she was fifteen. Or that Luke had stopped him from killing her.

"You okay?"

She dropped her phone on the counter, the noise echoing in the quiet kitchen. She hadn't heard Luke approach.

"Sorry." She plugged her phone into the charger, hands shaking. "Just thinking. My friend Randi called. I tried to call her back, but she didn't answer."

She was babbling and she knew it. Anything to hide her nervous reaction.

He wasn't fooled. He gently took her hand where it was fumbling with the cord. "It's all right. I will sleep here tonight on the couch. If anyone tries to break in, I'll stop them."

"But the Amish don't believe in violence. Not even to protect their families."

A dark shadow passed over his face. Was he regretting joining the church? The shadow lifted. "I won't shoot a gun. I won't start a fight. But I will place myself between you and LJ and anyone that tries to hurt you."

It sounded like a promise. Warmth drizzled down her spine at his words.

Then her guard went up.

She knew he meant well, but regardless of whether or not he remembered her, he had made his choice and joined the Amish church. That wasn't something he could undo. No matter how much he might want to stay and protect them, sooner or later he would have to leave them.

And no *Englisch* woman, not even the mother of his son, could go with him.

He didn't like the paleness in her cheeks. Nor the frantic edge in her voice. She wouldn't meet his gaze. What was going through her mind?

He put his finger to her chin to raise her eyes to his. In the back of his mind, he was shocked at his boldness. To touch a strange woman!

But this was no stranger. Even if his memory had never returned, this woman had married him and given him a son. He had a responsibility to them. Though he couldn't see any way for them to ever be a family again.

"Jennie."

Her eyes finally shot to his. He ignored the sizzle he felt at the connection; he searched her face for some clue to how she was really coping with all that had happened. His gut told him that she was one who tended to close herself off when bad things occurred. With her past, it would make sense that she would have trouble trusting.

Even him. Maybe especially him.

His heart ached at the thought. He shoved it aside. It was something he couldn't change.

"I'm fine, really," she responded to his unspoken question. "It's been a really hard day, and I don't like not having a plan. I like to know what to expect."

"You've always hated surprises," he replied, then stopped. How did he know that?

"Do you remember?"

He shook his head, sorry to see the hope draining from her lovely face. She really was a beautiful woman.

Stop it, he cautioned himself. *You don't have the right to notice that.*

"It's not that I remembered it. It's an impression that I had. I didn't realize I knew that about you until I said it."

When she turned and walked away, he wanted to call her back but had no idea what he planned on saying to her. It was a hopeless situation.

No, not hopeless. *Gott* was still in control, though it was difficult to see through the chaos swirling around them what His plan for them was. If only Luke could see the map that *Gott* intended them to follow.

Sighing, Luke prowled the perimeter of the living room, reading the spines of the books in the bookshelf and the labels on the DVDs, many of which seemed familiar to him. Had they watched any of these movies together? In his mind, he imagined snuggling with Jennie on the couch, laughing over a movie, possibly eating popcorn. It felt right, like they had done exactly that.

Had. It was in the past, and he had no reason to long for it now. His path had veered from the one he might have trod together with the beautiful brunette giggling softly with LJ. He tilted his head for a moment, rubbing his chest as the sound caught at him with the force of a fist striking him.

Lord, guide me. Give me the strength to protect them and to do Your will. Whether I want to do it or not.

Moving to the window, he shoved the curtains out of the way and peered down at the street below. The view was peaceful: trees covered with snow, the lawn a white blanket stretching out to the street. In the waning light, the snow almost seemed to glow. A snowplow drove past, its large plow scraping the road, creating a foot-tall barrier of snow along the side of the road.

Was someone out there now, watching them, planning another ambush? It was highly unlikely that whoever was behind the attacks was done. After all, there had been two attempts on Jennie's life today.

They should have called the police after the second attempt. It was a foreign thought to him. But Jennie wasn't Amish. She should have thought of it. Unless she didn't see the point. They couldn't identify the driver or the car. Would going to the police have changed things?

He let the curtains fall closed again.

The rest of the afternoon passed in tense silence. He tried to start up several conversations with Jennie, but sooner or later, one of them would lose the thread of the conversation. Dinner was a simple affair of grilled cheese sandwiches and tomato soup. LJ scrunched up his face when his mother poured a small amount of soup in his bowl, then grinned in delight when she placed a dill pickle spear on the plate next to his sandwich.

Luke shuddered, then glanced up, surprised when a chuckle gurgled out of Jennie.

"What?"

"You never did like pickles."

"They're unnatural."

A full belly laugh erupted from her. "Oh, my. You used to cringe when I would eat them straight out of the jar. Sometimes I'd do it just to see your reaction."

"You are a cruel woman." He fought the urge to grin, attempting to school his face into a stern expression. It probably looked ridiculous.

She winked, then dropped her eyes. No doubt, she recalled the seriousness of their situation.

After dinner, Jennie rose to give LJ his bath and put him to bed.

"I'll take care of the dishes," Luke offered.

She raised an eyebrow. "You used to avoid doing dishes like the plague."

He grimaced. "I don't like doing dishes, true, but it's a job that has to be done, ain't so?"

Her nose wrinkled up. "You even sound Amish now. When we met, you went out of your way to sound American."

"Englisch," he corrected. Still, he frowned. "I remember feeling rebellious as a teenager. I don't anymore."

"Obviously."

He couldn't tell if she was being critical or stating a fact.

"Come on, LJ. Bath time."

"Yippee!" The four-year-old hopped down from his seat. "With bubbles?"

"With bubbles."

Luke found himself smiling at his son's exuberance. The smile faded as he contemplated the situation while doing the dishes. How would he protect them? He knew what Steve Curtis looked like, but by now it was clear that Steve had other people coming after Jennie. It could be anyone they passed on the street. It could even be people she knew and trusted.

Although, she didn't seem like a person who trusted that many people. Her mother may have been partly to blame for that. It was hard to imagine a mother abandoning her children the way Jennie's parent had. The horrible things she'd endured while in the foster care system couldn't have helped. And then Steve had attacked her. His lips tightened at the thought of the young girl she had once been suffering, with no one to listen.

An image of Jennie flashed in his mind, hair in a disheveled ponytail, tears tracking down a dirty, bruised face. He blinked and the image was gone. Was it a memory? His heart hurt for that girl.

And he marveled at the strong woman she'd grown into. Jennie might have suffered, but she was certainly not a victim. She'd raised a smart, happy son. A son who had no idea that the world could be a dangerous place.

His son.

Danke, Gott, for keeping them safe. Help me protect them.

Thirty minutes later, a clean LJ rushed down the hall to hug him good-night. "Night, Daddy! I'm going to sleep in Mama's room tonight."

"I don't want to let him out of my sight," Jennie explained. "Is that silly?"

"I think it's smart," Luke said, "after the day you had."

She tossed him a quick, weary smile, before leading LJ off to bed. She was back fifteen minutes later, her arms stacked with bedding for him.

"I have extra blankets in the hall closet if you get cold."

"Danke." He took the linens from her, almost flinching when their fingers met. The tingle he felt at the touch was not good, definitely not something he should enjoy. He couldn't help it, though. *She is my wife, even if I don't remember her.*

The thought brought no comfort.

He set about putting the sheet on the couch. Leaving his boots and his hat near the door, he stretched out, determined to sleep.

An hour later, he was still wide-awake, listening to

the cars drive up and down the road. Was Steve in one of those cars?

At about one in the morning, he woke with a shout, the dream about being caught in a fire, trying to get to Jennie and LJ fading. Tossing the blanket aside, he jumped up from the couch and went to look out the window to check for any perils again. He couldn't see anything through the thick haze of fresh falling snow. The windows shook with the force of the wind. He laid one hand flat against the pane. It was ice-cold. His breath misted the glass.

Uneasy, he walked down the hall. He could hear LJ's light snore coming from Jennie's room. A second later, he smiled when he heard a soft noise inside. She'd sneezed in her sleep.

She had asthma, he recalled.

Frustrated, he willed himself to recall more. Nothing came.

Finally, he returned to the couch.

It was going to be a long night.

FIVE

"Mama, I don't want to sleep in your room anymore. Your walls are scary."

Jennie sighed. LJ had woken her up out of a sound sleep. Her walls were scary? She looked around her room, trying to imagine how it looked to a four-year-old. Ahh. There were shadows on her walls. She sometimes left the blinds open a few inches.

Getting out of bed, she closed the plastic slats, eradicating the looming shadows on her wall.

"Is that better, sweetie?"

"Yeah," LJ said, dragging the word out.

"But?"

"I want my light."

Of course.

"I'll be right back." Jennie turned on her bedside light, so that he wouldn't get scared, then quickly went to his room to collect his Scooby-Doo night-light. A minute later, she was plugging it in.

"Okay?"

"Okay."

Finally. She tucked the covers around him before getting in on the other side of the bed. It took her a while to fall asleep. Her mind refused to accept that it was time to slow down and instead kept running over the events of the day.

Almost as shocking as Steve's escape was Luke's return. Her brain couldn't get over the change in him. When she had met him, he'd kept his curly hair short and typically wore faded blue jeans and T-shirts. If it was cold, then flannel shirts were his main defense against the weather. To see him looking so much more mature than the man she'd married, and staring at her with nearly no recognition, it was like hearing he'd died all over again. And the way he dressed! She hadn't exaggerated when she told him that he used to go out of his way to appear *Englisch*. Anything he could do to blend in with her world he'd do. She knew he had often rebelled against what was expected when they were younger. Part of that might have had to do with the fact that he and his father clashed so frequently. That was why he'd left the Amish world. Today, she could see that he was completely comfortable in his choice to join the Amish world.

Of course, he hadn't known about her. That would have made a difference. She knew it would have. Maybe if she'd insisted he wear a wedding ring, he would have at least known he was married and come searching for her. At the time, though, she hadn't argued when he'd said wearing a ring, or jewelry of any kind, made him uncomfortable.

Jennie huffed and flopped over on her other side. This was doing no good. It didn't matter how many times she thought about what might have happened. Nothing would change. She'd still have been alone for the past five years.

He was here now, her mind whispered. Yeah, but for how long?

Finally, she drifted into an uneasy sleep.

Jennie sat up in bed, her senses on full alert. The room was dark still. What had awakened her?

Reaching out a trembling hand, she patted LJ's warm body. She could feel the steady rise and fall of his little chest as he breathed deeply, still sound asleep. Relief seeped down into her soul.

He was safe.

A quick glance at the digital clock glowing on her nightstand told her it was just past four in the morning. Not quite time to rise. She normally didn't get up until six.

But something had awakened her. Silently, she pushed her covers away and slid off her side of the bed, taking care not to make too much movement. She didn't want to disturb LJ. Once he woke up, there'd be no getting him back to sleep. She really had no desire to rise for the day before dawn. It had taken her so long to get to sleep in the first place.

She pushed her feet into the slippers she kept tucked under the edge of the bed before padding out to the hall. Once there, she paused, listening. She could hear the wind wailing outside and shivered in response. Moving to the thermostat, she turned the heat up a notch. Normally, she wouldn't, but she felt bad about Luke sleeping on the couch. The living room always tended to be a little drafty, and that couch couldn't be comfortable.

She went into the kitchen to get a drink of water, careful to keep the glass from clinking. On her way back to the bedroom, she paused.

What was that noise she heard? It came from outside. She went into her room and tried to look out her window. Her window faced away from the street. There were no streetlamps to illuminate the ground below. In fact, it was impossible to see anything moving about in the inky blackness outside.

There was a large tree right outside. Its branches stretched up to her second floor window and beyond. Sometimes they scraped against the windows. She'd probably heard that and, in her paranoia, was overreacting.

Kicking off her slippers, she crawled back into her bed, pulling the covers up over her shoulders. Lying on her side, she placed her arm around LJ.

Everything was fine, she told herself. She was well, LJ was here at her side and Luke was just in the next room. Closing her eyes, she tried to will herself back to sleep. It was hard with her heart running like a freight train.

Thump. Scratch.

Her eyes shot open. That was no tree branch. Something was outside her apartment.

She hurried out of bed. Should she wake Luke? There was no way she was going to be like one of those women in a horror movie and go investigate the noise by herself. Not when she already knew someone was out to kill her.

Another scratch made up her mind. This one sounded like it was right outside LJ's room. Flipping on the hallway light, she ran to the bed and grabbed her son. Picking him up, she carried him as quickly as she could to the living room and deposited him on the love seat.

Luke was sleeping on his back, one arm flung over his head.

"Luke!" She ran to him and shook his shoulder. "Luke! Wake up."

Faster than she would have believed possible, he bolted upright, knocking her over. He yelled out in Pennsylvania Dutch. She didn't understand the words, but by then, he seemed to be aware of his surroundings. He bounded to his feet, helping her to stand even as his eyes scanned the living room. His posture relaxed when his eyes fell on LJ still asleep on the love seat.

"Are you all right? What's going on?"

She wrapped her arms around her middle, chilled despite the fact that the living room was now a toasty seventy degrees.

"I heard something. I thought it might have been a tree scraping along the side of the apartment. But then I heard another sound, coming from outside LJ's room. There's no way it could have been a tree branch."

She didn't say anything else. Luke was already headed down the hall. She wanted to call him back. What if someone was in there, and he got ambushed?

"Luke," she called out, her voice a raspy whisper.

When he didn't respond, she grabbed her cell phone and lowered herself to the floor in front of the love seat where her son was sitting. She wanted to be ready to call 911 at a moment's notice.

Luke stepped into LJ's bedroom. The light filtering in from the hall illuminated much of the room, casting eerie shadows on the wall. He stood for a moment, allowing his eyes to scan the room. Nothing stood out as being out of place.

Jennie had heard noises from outside. Striding over to the window, he opened the blinds. There was nothing moving outside. Casting his eyes down, he froze.

Up against the side of the building, propped right against the windowsill leading into his son's room, was a ladder.

"Jennie," he called out softly.

Within seconds, she was in the doorway. She seemed to glow, silhouetted against the soft white light from the hall. For a brief moment, he was trapped, an image of her in a long white gown flashing through his mind.

When it vanished, he blinked.

"Did you find something?" she asked.

He pulled himself back from the sense of loss suddenly engulfing him. Unable to speak, he nodded and pointed to the window, giving himself time to recover.

Brow furrowed in confusion, she stepped to his side and looked out. When she sucked in a breath, he knew she'd seen the ladder.

Hoping his voice was under control, he asked, "Was that there earlier?"

He wasn't surprised when she shook her head. "No. I'll bet when he leaned it against the window, that was the thud I heard."

"Do you want to call the police?" He was normally reluctant to take that course of action, but when it came to Jennie and LJ, he found he was more than willing to do whatever was necessary to keep them safe.

"Oh, yeah. Definitely." Her chin quivered before she steadied herself. She was so pale. "Luke, if I hadn't heard that noise, and if LJ had been sleeping in here…"

"Hey." Luke pulled her into his arms and held her tight against his chest. "Neither of those things happened. You can't torture yourself with what might have happened. You're safe, LJ's safe and I'm here. We're going to call the police now, and then we'll go from there. *Jah?*"

Her only response was to nod her head against his chest.

He wanted to stay in this position, but knew he needed to let her go. Just one more second.

She pulled back. Reluctantly, he opened his arms and watched as she stepped away.

"I'm good." She surveyed the window once more before spinning around and striding from the room. He could hear her voice a moment later on the phone with the police. "They'll be here in under ten, Luke."

"I'm going to clean up."

He gathered his bag and went into the bathroom. He arrived back in the living room to find that LJ had woken up and Jennie was opening the front door and standing out of the way so the police trooper who had come to check out the situation could enter. Trooper Carter looked around and waved at LJ, who was sitting in front of the television, watching a video Jennie had put on for him.

LJ waved back and took a bite of toast his mother must have made him while Luke was in the bathroom, his eyes back on the screen.

Luke looked at Jennie and raised his eyebrow.

She nodded her head in LJ's direction. "He isn't allowed to watch TV unless it's a special occasion, so he's probably not going to move from that spot until the video's done."

He approved, he decided. LJ didn't need to know how worried his parents were. Or how close he had come—

Nee. He hadn't let Jennie go there earlier, so neither would he. He turned his eyes back to the trooper talking with her.

"You woke when you heard something?" Carter was saying.

"Yes, I wasn't sure what, but it was a strange sound. One I had never heard before. When I heard another sound coming from the direction of *his* room…" she lowered her voice and discreetly pointed at the four-year-old engrossed in cartoons "… I came and got Luke. He was sleeping on the couch."

Carter turned his gaze to Luke, who picked up the narrative. "There was nothing in the room, and I couldn't see anyone outside. It was still dark. That's when I saw the ladder."

Carter's eyes sharpened. "Ladder? You better show me."

Jennie's gaze flashed to LJ.

Luke touched her hand. "Jennie, why don't you stay with LJ and I'll take Trooper Carter back?"

Relief flickered across her face and she nodded. He understood. She didn't trust LJ to be safe alone in a room in his own home anymore. The idea saddened him.

"This way." Luke led Carter down the hall and stood back while the trooper examined LJ's room. Carter pulled a pair of latex gloves over his hands and opened the window before peering at the screen. He pushed on the bottom of it. The entire screen came off and crashed into the bushes directly below the window.

That shouldn't have happened.

Carter looked out of the window and whistled. Luke moved closer. "What?"

The trooper stood up, closing the outer window. Motioning for Luke to follow, he returned to where Jennie stood waiting at the end of the hall. She had a clear view of LJ and the men coming toward her.

"You found something."

There was certainty, and a tremor of dread, in her soft voice.

"The storm window had been removed. It was lying on the ground, broken. Whether he dropped it or stepped on it when he fled, it's hard to say. The screen fell when I touched it. He must have been removing it."

She dropped her head in her hands. "Oh! He was so close."

"I noticed the lock on the window is ancient. It wouldn't have taken much for him to have gotten past it."

Jennie made no protest when Luke slipped an arm around her shoulders to comfort her. In fact, she leaned in, letting him take some of her weight. "I had no idea they were in such bad shape."

"Well, something must have scared whoever it was away. Did you come into the room?"

She shook her head. "No. I heard the noise, got LJ and brought him out here, then I woke up Luke."

"You didn't turn on the light or anything?"

"Just the hall light."

Luke spoke up. "The bedroom door was half open. Was it that Deets guy, do you think? Could the hall light have been enough to scare him away?"

"Could have been him. And turning on the light might have scared him off." The trooper looked at Jennie. "Mrs. Beiler, is there anywhere that you can stay for the time being? Until we catch this person, I don't recommend you remain here. However, if you are determined to stay, I think I can offer you some protection. I can see if the department could have a cruiser drive by several times a day."

"I don't know. There are so many people in and out of the building." She paused.

"There is that. Also, your apartment is on the side of the building. It would be harder to see from the street. Which brings me back to my first question. Is there somewhere else you could hole up for a while until we catch this guy?"

She floundered, tears shimmering in her brown eyes. "I don't know. My brother is away. I have a key to his place. Maybe we could stay there."

Trooper Carter appeared to consider the idea for a moment. Finally, he shook his head. "I don't think that's the best plan. If you're right, and your stepfather is behind these events, it's possible he may look for you at your brother's house."

Her shoulders sagged beneath Luke's arm. He tightened his hold for an instant, a silent reminder that he was there for her. He agreed with the trooper. If his sister Theresa was in trouble, she came to either he or Raymond for help. He had no doubt Steve would search for her at Aiden's place.

She couldn't stay here. Jennie hadn't been able to identify the man who had nearly run her over, nor could she identify the man that had tried to get in through the window. It could have been Steve, though Luke didn't think so. It seemed unlikely that the man would have been able to travel this far already. It was almost two hundred miles on foot. Even if he had a driver, it appeared he had recruited others. There was no way to know how many people were involved. Jennie could be talking with one of the man's henchmen and not even know it.

"I know where you could stay," Luke stated. "You could stay at *Onkel* Jed's *haus*."

Jennie blinked at him, her face blank for a moment. "Your uncle wouldn't want some stranger interrupting his life."

"*Onkel* Jed is not a stranger to you. You've met him before. And unlike me, he has never lost his memory."

Carter's eyebrows climbed nearly to his receding hairline.

"It's been years since I saw him. He had no idea that we were getting married. You sort of broke all connection with your family at that time," Jennie said.

Was that regret he heard?

"He might not have known about us, but he is a *gut* man. I know he would want to help if he could."

"It might not be a bad idea," Trooper Carter broke in. "You have to go somewhere. If the man's willing to help, and if he's someone that no one would think of, it's a good plan. I would need the address. To keep in touch and to check in with you."

"I can give you that." Now that the idea had been accepted, Luke actually liked the idea of her coming to stay with his family. At the same time, he wondered if it was a horrible idea, having her staying so close. He could stay elsewhere, put distance between them.

That was what he would do. He would see Jennie and LJ safely to his *onkel* Jed's *haus*, then he would find another place to stay. Somewhere close enough to keep in touch daily, but far enough away to help him resist the lure of this lovely woman.

He needed to start distancing himself now. Casually, he dropped the arm that was still about her shoulders. It hung at his side, feeling empty and useless. He ignored the temptation to put it back.

He missed them already.

SIX

She didn't like the empty look that flickered over Luke's face. Wherever he had gone in his mind, it was a dark place. She wished he hadn't moved away. His touch had been comforting and warm.

"Luke." She reached out and touched his arm. When he stiffened, his face tightening as if in pain, she dropped her hand like it had been burned. Her face flushed in embarrassment. Then anger stirred.

"Get me that address," Trooper Carter was saying.

"Do you have paper?" Luke asked. "I can write it down for you."

"If you know it, just tell it to me. I'll put it in my phone."

Luke rattled off the address from memory.

"Phone number?"

"Um, my *onkel* is Amish. He doesn't have a phone number."

Carter waved that away. "He must have a business phone."

"*Jah*. I don't know that number. I've never had a reason to use it. We'll have to contact you with it later."

Jennie stared at Luke. "So we'll just appear on his doorstep?" That seemed rude.

"He's my *onkel*. It won't matter what time of day or night we show up."

"Whatever you do, do it quick." Carter turned to leave. "I suggest you leave ASAP."

The next forty minutes were a flurry of activity as Jennie packed for her and LJ and Luke kept the child entertained and out of the way. As they were packing everything into her car, she had a thought. She had no way of knowing how long they'd be gone. Grabbing her purse, she retrieved her wallet. Just as she feared. It was almost empty.

"We're going to have to stop at the bank."

Luke stopped in the middle of loading her bags into the trunk. "Now? Can it wait?"

"Nope. Sorry. I'm out of cash, and I'm not comfortable relying on my bank card."

He sighed. "*Jah*, I can understand that. It is always best to use money."

Luke had never liked the idea of bank cards or credit cards. Was that his personality or his Amish upbringing? Not that it mattered. She shrugged and finished buckling LJ into his booster seat and got in behind the wheel. She backed out of her parking space. It was a good thing the plows had already come through. The roads, although clear, were still slippery. Frustration bit at her as she drove. Her instinct told her to move, but caution made her keep her speed well below the speed limit. She hated driving in the winter.

"Do you miss driving?"

Where had that question come from? But now that she had asked, she found she really wanted to know.

"*Nee*. I don't remember driving, so I can't miss it."

She nodded. "You used to complain that I drove too fast."

He tossed her a quick smile. "I still don't like being in a car when it's going too fast. I use a driver when I need to, but I prefer the simple pleasure of driving a buggy. I can think better and take time to appreciate the world *Gott* created."

Jennie squirmed in her seat. She wasn't sure she wanted to bring God into their conversation, not when He hadn't protected them.

Or maybe He had.

Her glance slid to Luke. His appearance had been timely. She couldn't deny it.

She tossed her head, trying to dislodge the idea. It was so disconcerting to think that after she'd been ignoring God for years, He was still reaching out to be a part of her life.

They arrived at the bank just as the doors were being unlocked. She'd forgotten how early in the morning it still was. She'd been up for so long it felt like it should be nearing lunchtime.

The reason why she'd been up so early made her stomach clench.

No time to think about that now. She parked the car in front of the bank and shut off the engine. Luke looked at her in surprise.

"I thought you'd go to the ATM machine." He pointed to the drive-thru line.

She shrugged. "I don't trust the things. Working with technology the way I do on a daily basis, I've seen too many systems get hacked."

He looked thoughtful but didn't argue. Instead,

he unbuckled his seat belt and opened his door. She climbed out her side and popped open the back door.

"Let's go." She grabbed up LJ and the three of them went into the lobby. They were the first customers for the day. As she stepped up to the counter, Luke wandered over to the small sitting area on the left, looking over the complimentary coffee and tea selection.

The pretty clerk at the counter, Brenda, greeted them. "Good morning, Jennie. LJ."

"Morning, Brenda." Jennie kept her voice light and friendly. She didn't like the way Brenda was looking at Luke. He was a handsome man, and the clerk was definitely noticing.

"Are you going on a trip? Or just getting ready to go Christmas shopping, something like that?" Brenda's chatty voice didn't disguise the avid curiosity in her face. She wasn't asking out of politeness.

"Something like that," she hedged. Sudden suspicion tugged at Jennie, cautioning her to mind how much information she gave out. Could Brenda be involved? She immediately scoffed at herself. Brenda was harmless. Chatty and somewhat flaky, she was well-known in town for her love of gossip.

Efficiently, Brenda counted the money back to Jennie. Thanking her, Jennie shoved the money into a bank envelope and put it in the purse slung across her body. She zipped it and smiled at Brenda, preparing to leave.

"So, Jennie." The clerk leaned closer, pitching her voice low. Her heavy floral perfume hit Jennie's nose, causing it to itch. She was afraid to breathe in too deep, fearing the thick scent would send her into an asthma attack. "I can't help but notice that good-looking man you came in with. Who is he?"

Jennie backed away, keeping her smile in place with an effort. "Just an old friend. Look, I'd love to chat, but we're on a schedule today."

As she backed away, she nearly ran into Pete Walsh. Pete worked at the local auto parts store. He'd asked her out a few times. Jennie had always refused, politely, telling him she had no time for dating. Something about the way his expression always seemed to border on a leer had made her uncomfortable. He was eyeing Luke, his expression bitter.

"You won't go out with me, but you'll hang out with some Amish dude?" he asked.

"It's not what you think," she began.

The ringing of her phone cut her off. Randi. Finally.

"Hey, Randi," Jennie said, turning away from Pete. "What's up?"

"Jennie. You have to come over. Now. I found something you need to see."

Click. She'd disconnected.

"Jennie?" Luke had returned to her side and was gently taking her elbow and leading her toward the door. LJ was clinging to his other hand.

Jennie looked around. Both Brenda and Pete were still watching. It was like being in a fishbowl. Everywhere she turned, someone was looking at her. Despite her dislike of ATMs, she wished she'd used one today.

She left the building, not trusting herself to talk until they were back in her car. Once the doors were shut behind them, she turned to Luke. "My friend Randi has been trying to call me for the past day. We've been playing phone tag." She bit at her lip. "I haven't been able to shake the feeling that she's in trouble. Anyway, she called while I was in the bank."

"I was there. I heard her call."

"Well, she said she found something I needed to see. Her voice sounded weird. I can't explain it. I know something's wrong with her. Is it all right if we stop by her place for a few minutes before heading to your uncle's?"

For a moment, she thought he'd refuse. It might have delayed them, but she had a nagging sense that something was really wrong with Randi.

"*Jah*, we can stop. If you're worried about your friend, then let's go."

She nodded, then pulled out of the bank parking lot. With each minute, her tension ratcheted higher. The twenty-minute drive seemed to take an hour.

Twice she wondered if they were being followed. When the cars turned off each time, she scolded herself for letting her paranoia get the best of her.

When they arrived at the house, she pulled into the drive. The fresh snow was marred by tire tracks. There were footprints leading to the garage, which was closed.

She frowned.

"It's not like her to have the curtains still closed at this time of day." She glanced down at the clock. "It's almost ten in the morning. She's always up and about by seven at the latest."

"What do you want to do?"

She looked back at LJ. "Honey, Mama's going to go knock on Miss Randi's door. You stay here with Daddy, all right?"

"'Kay, Mama!" LJ shouted, kicking his feet. The boy had tons of energy; he was always moving.

Luke wasn't looking happy. "I don't know. Maybe I should go and you stay here."

"Nah. Look, if anything seems wrong, I'll call you over." She shut the car door before he could protest any further. Striding up the walk to the front door of Randi's house, she passed the large picture window. The sheers were drawn, but behind them she could dimly see Randi's Christmas tree, still lit up and twinkling. That was so like Randi. The woman loved Christmas and anything sparkly. While Jennie would always fret about the cost of leaving on extra lights, Randi left the tree lights on 24/7 when she was home.

Well, at least I know she's here, Jennie mused. Moving past the tree, she tromped to the steps, trying to appear more confident than she actually felt. Randi had never taken this long to respond to a message from her.

The front stairs hadn't been shoveled yet, but it was still early. She stepped carefully, grimacing as snow brushed the top of her short boots and fell in. Great. Now she would have to deal with wet feet, too.

She knocked sharply on the front door. "Randi? It's Jennie."

Nothing. She waited a moment, then tried again.

Where was she? She raised her hand to pound on the door a third time, then paused. What was that noise? It almost sounded like a small dog barking inside, except she knew that Randi hated dogs. They terrified her, no matter how small they were. Leaning in, Jennie heard the noise again.

It wasn't barking, it was the sound of someone groaning in agony! Urgently, she yanked on the screen door. It wouldn't open. Randi always locked the door when she went to bed.

Without a thought for the snow, Jennie turned and leaped down the stairs, slipping when her boots hit the drive. She caught herself before she fell and raced back to the car as fast as she could in the snow.

"I think she's hurt," she panted. "I can hear her inside, but the door is locked!"

Luke was already getting out of the car. "Can we call anyone?"

"No time!" She ran to the garage.

Randi had given her the code once before. What was it? Jennie got it the third time she tried, and the door lifted. Suddenly, Luke was there with LJ in his arms.

"You take him," he said, handing the child to her. She hugged her son close and followed Luke to the door that led into the house. It was unlocked.

Moving inside, she gasped at the wreckage of her friend's family room. In front of her was the low island separating the room from the kitchen. She could hear moaning beyond the counter. Stepping around it, she gasped.

Randi was lying on the floor, beaten and bruised.

This was no accident. Someone had gotten here before them.

Luke shoved LJ and Jennie back. "Don't let him see this."

She was already moving away, talking quietly to the child, distracting him by being silly. When he heard LJ giggle, his shoulders loosened slightly. The boy hadn't seen the injured woman.

Luke moved around to where Randi lay. Her swollen eyes opened when he squatted down near her. She whimpered in fear. He held out a hand, as if he were calming an injured animal.

"Hush. I'm not here to hurt you. I'm with Jennie."

"Jennie." Her voice was little more than a whisper.

"That's right. She's keeping LJ away. Can you tell me who did this to you?" Another thought occurred to him. "Is he still in the *haus*?"

She licked her lips. "He's gone."

Luke nodded. "Can I help you get up?"

Randi closed her eyes. "Give me a few seconds. I'm feeling nauseous."

"Okay. I'll be right back."

He stepped away from the injured woman and moved to Jennie's side. She looked at him with huge eyes.

"She thinks her attacker is gone," he murmured. "I want to check the *haus* and make sure."

"Be careful."

"I will." He left them and made his way around the *haus*, checking each room and the basement. There were no signs of anyone else in the place. On his way back to the kitchen area, he saw some crayons and a coloring book in the home office area. Thinking of LJ, he gathered them up and brought them with him. When he returned, he handed the crayons and the coloring book to Jennie, then went back over to Randi.

Behind them, he heard some scraping furniture. Standing, he saw that Jennie had settled LJ on a chair at the dining room table, the coloring book and crayons in front of him. The little boy was furiously coloring, his tongue sticking out between his teeth in concentration. A moment later, Jennie joined Luke, her eyes dry, although he knew her heart had to be aching as she looked on her friend.

"Can you sit up now?" Luke asked. "How bad are you hurt?"

"I think so. I don't feel like I'm going to throw up

anymore. Help me." Her voice was stronger then before, although raspy. "I want to try and sit. I'm sore, but I don't think anything's broken."

Together, Jennie and Luke helped Randi to sit up. When it appeared all her bones were intact, they helped her to stand. She moved slowly to the recliner near the door and sank into it, holding her breath on the way down.

"Oh, Randi, what happened?" Jennie asked at last.

"It was Morgan," the woman gasped out.

Jennie's jaw dropped.

Luke was lost. "Morgan? Who's Morgan?"

Randi closed her eyes briefly. "Morgan's my brother. Well, my half brother. After I left foster care, we kept in contact. He's spent some time in and out of jail for the past ten years. When he got out five months ago, he had no place to go so I let him stay here."

Jennie didn't look surprised by that. "You always had a soft spot for him."

"You never liked him."

Luke watched, fascinated, as a tide of pink swept up over Jennie's face.

"It's not—"

Randi choked out a weak laugh. "Oh, I'm not blaming you. You might have been smarter than me. You always said he was trouble waiting to happen." Her voice cracked and a sob burst out.

Jennie hurried to embrace her friend. Luke turned his head, wanting to give them some privacy in the small space. *Ach*, this was awkward. He went over and sat with LJ, listening with one ear to the murmured conversation behind him.

"What're you working on?" He reached out and ruffled the curls on the boy's head.

"I'm drawing a picture of my doggy."

Luke's eyebrows rose. "Your doggy? I didn't know you had a doggy."

LJ didn't look up from his important task. "Not yet. I will, though. I'm going to call him Buster."

"Why Buster?"

He sensed Jennie's warmth at his back. The scent of vanilla wrapped itself around him, reminding him of home and security. "Buster's the name of your friend Joey's dog, honey. We can't have a dog in our apartment."

Clearly, this was an old familiar discussion.

He glanced back. "Where'd Randi go?"

Jennie glanced at him out of the corner of her eyes. "She said she had something to show me. That's the reason she'd called me earlier. Morgan showed up just after we hung up. When he saw what she'd found, he went ballistic and attacked her. Then he'd swiped her phone so she couldn't call for help. I think he thought she'd die. She didn't tell him we were on the way."

"Did you ever tell her about Steve?" He kept his question vague, not wanting LJ's innocent ears to hear about his *mamm* getting attacked.

She bit her lip. "I told her about what happened when I was eleven and how I ended up in foster care. She has no idea about the other time, when I was fifteen, and I doubt she guessed. I took great care to pretend that it never happened. You're the only I've ever told. I might not have even told you, except that you were there immediately after."

He bowed his head, a memory of her battered face and blood-soaked clothes edging its way into his mind.

"Luke?" Her hand touched his.

"I remember. Not everything. Just an image." He grabbed her hand briefly to reassure himself that she was well before dropping it.

She drew in a harsh breath.

He returned to the subject they'd been discussing. "How could that and her brother be connected? Did she ever meet Steve?"

"Never. I asked the same question. She said she'd need me to see it to understand."

It made no sense to him.

Randi interrupted anything else they might have said. She shuffled back into the room, obviously still in pain. Her face was pale as she dropped a shoebox on the counter. Several photographs spilled out of the box. Jennie bent to grab one that had slid off the counter and floated to the carpet.

As she stood up, she flipped the picture over. Luke noticed all the color leeched from her face, leaving her complexion ashen. Rushing to her side, he placed his arm around her as she swayed slightly. He met her gaze but doubted she was actually seeing him. She'd gone somewhere else in her mind.

"Jennie!" he said firmly.

She blinked. Color flowed back into her cheeks, though she still didn't look like herself. When she pushed the picture into his hand, his fingers closed around it automatically.

He gave her one last look to make sure she was steady before taking a look at the picture that had such a shocking effect on her.

It was a picture of Jennie, staring out her window in her apartment. Heat started to swirl in his gut. He breathed in through his nose to keep calm. Setting the picture aside, he reached into the box to look at another picture, and another. The heat was spreading, a wildfire of rage swirling inside him. He couldn't speak without spewing the anger out.

Morgan must have spent years gathering pictures of Jennie. Some showed Jennie holding a younger LJ, but some of the pictures were recent.

"My brother is a photography nut," Randi said, her whole body sagging with sorrow. "I thought maybe he'd found something useful to do with his time. He even has a dark room upstairs, although I would guess nowadays he takes digital pics and has them uploaded on his laptop. I was cleaning out a closet in the basement yesterday and I found these and called Jennie immediately. I didn't expect him home until tomorrow. When he came in this morning and saw me holding them, he went berserk."

"I'm surprised he left these with you," Jennie said.

Randi hesitated. "He took most of them. These were the ones that were left on the bottom of the closet."

"These were the ones left?" Luke repeated, amazed and sickened. How many pictures had the man taken of Jennie?

"Why?" Jennie's voice trembled. "Why would Morgan be taking pictures of me? I've never done anything to him."

Luke didn't like what he was hearing. "Do you have a picture of Morgan? I think I need to see what he looks like."

Randi sighed. "Not a recent one. There's a picture of him and a buddy on a fishing trip on the kitchen counter. He's the one with mullet."

Luke walked to the counter to look at the picture. Morgan Griggs looked ordinary enough. Dark hair, dark eyes, wide smile.

"Is he obsessed with Jennie?" Luke asked. "I've heard that stalking is a serious problem in the *Englisch* world."

Jennie's mouth dropped open. "I can't believe he would be interested in me, even as a stalker."

"He's not. I think he's working with Steve, your stepfather."

The silence that followed that statement lasted for nearly a minute. Luke couldn't imagine how such a thing could happen.

"Where would they have met?" Jennie demanded. "I never told Morgan about my stepfather."

Randi glanced away. "That's my fault. When Morgan and I were younger, he was making fun of you. You'd made him mad by rebuffing him. I made the mistake of telling him that you'd had a rough life and an abusive stepfather. You'd told me that he had attacked you when you a kid, and your brother had saved you. I knew that you'd testified against him before. It wasn't hard to figure out the rest."

Luke made no protest when Jennie latched onto his arm. Randi's comment didn't bode well.

"What do you mean?" Jennie asked sharply.

Now Randi looked annoyed. "Oh, come on, Jennie. I knew that you were testifying against him. So did Morgan. You never said why, and the newspapers didn't release your name, but we all knew what crimes they listed against him. When Morgan went to jail the first time, he ended up in the same prison that Steve Curtis was in. I'm not sure how the two of them became friends. Morgan didn't confide in me. My guess is that when Morgan was released, Steve must have convinced him to keep tabs on you. It's the only thing that makes sense."

Luke didn't like the lost expression on Jennie's face. "How many people have been watching us?" she cried out suddenly, her eyes haunted.

"What do you mean?" Randi frowned.

Luke winced at the bruises slowly darkening on her face. He had no tolerance for any man who would strike a woman or child.

Jennie scrubbed the heels of her hands over her eyes. "There was someone taking pictures of LJ at his pre-school and now this. Steve has obviously been planning for some time. I don't know how to fight an enemy if I don't know who it is." When she raised her head, her eyes were red. "Randi, you have to get out of here. It's not safe for you. Come with us."

Jennie reached out and grabbed her friend's hand, her face imploring her to agree. Luke could see the moment Randi made her decision.

"I'll come. Let me pack a few things."

"What's that noise?" Jennie frowned. "And do you smell something?"

"It's coming from the garage," Luke said, walking toward the door they'd entered. "Leave the room, just in case." He waited until Jennie had taken the other two into the hallway. He opened the door, surprising a man pouring gasoline over the firewood stacked along the inside wall. He recognized the man from the picture on Randi's counter. It was Morgan. When Morgan saw Luke, he rushed toward him. Instinctively, Luke backed up. Then Morgan threw the gasoline can inside the house. Liquid poured from the container, spilling all over the carpet and the drapes. Luke moved to slam the door. Too late. The other man pulled a highway flare from his back pocket, gave it a hard twist and threw the burning flare into the room.

Luke bolted from the room and joined the women and LJ in the hall.

"Quick! We can't get out this way! Head to the front door."

By this time, the flames were flickering up the drapes on the family room window and spreading across the carpet.

They had minutes. Luke was once again inside his darkest fear.

But this time, if he failed, the child he had just met and the wife he was only starting to remember would pay the ultimate price.

SEVEN

Smoke was filling the house. Luke heard Jennie and LJ coughing.

"Head to the living room. We'll leave by the front door," Luke yelled. He swept LJ up in his arms, pushing the child's nose against his shirt.

They were almost to the front door when the back of the house exploded. Randi bounced off the wall next to him. She fell hard. He had no idea if she was even alive.

Where was Jennie? Luke turned, and brushed against her. She was alive and keeping pace with him.

Panic was clouding his mind. He shook his head to clear it away. He needed to think. He was not a teenager stuck inside a burning building, helpless. He was a grown man with a responsibility to his family. He was the only hope Jennie and LJ had.

Nee. Gott was their hope. Luke was the instrument *Gott* could use. If he let Him.

Please, Gott. Use me to save their lives. Help me keep my mind steady on Your purpose.

"Jennie, LJ, drop to the floor. It's safer. The air is cleaner." He set LJ down and was gratified to see both of them get down immediately.

Jennie was overtaken with a fit of coughing. When she got her cough under control, Luke could hear her wheeze when she breathed. A new fear entered his mind. If she had an asthma attack now, it could be bad.

Something in the other room crashed to the ground. LJ screamed. A blast of heat hit them as the flames seared up the wood of the front door and the wall behind them.

"I'm scared, Daddy!" LJ started to sob. It broke Luke's heart to hear it, but he needed to get the situation under control.

"LJ, I need you to be a big boy. Jennie, LJ, crawl toward the front window."

They started to crawl on hands and knees. Luke struggled to drag Randi behind him. He couldn't hold in his own coughs as he breathed in some of the smoke.

"Faster!" he shouted. *Dear Lord, let us make it.*

The Christmas tree was blocking the large picture window, their only hope for escape. Luke dropped Randi and ran to the window, throwing the tree aside. Ornaments and glass balls fell to the floor and shattered. The lights went out as the cord was torn from the electrical socket. Luke swiveled his head from side to side as he searched for something to break the window. His gaze landed on an umbrella stand near the wall. A large cane was sticking out of it.

Surging forward, he yanked the cane out of the stand. His eyes were watering from the smoke. He blinked to clear them and smashed the cane through the window. The glass shattered, raining down on the floor. The broken shards looked like hundreds of diamonds, and they crunched under his heavy boots.

Sweeping the cane back and forth, he broke off as

much glass from the window frame as he could, then pulled up a heavy braided area rug and threw it over the remaining jagged edges.

"LJ, come here, son."

LJ ran to his father, his face drenched in tears.

"I'm going to lower you through the window. Go stand by the tree outside and wait for your mama," Luke told him.

LJ's chin wobbled, but he nodded his understanding. Careful not to bring the boy too close to any of the shards, Luke reached him past the window wreckage and dropped him on the snow below.

"Go, LJ. To the tree!"

LJ stood up and ran to the tree, his face white with fear.

"Jennie."

She was already at his side. He grasped her hand and assisted her over the ledge. Their eyes met for a single instant before she was out the window. The moment her feet touched the ground, she ran to LJ and gathered him in her arms.

They were safe.

By this time, the smoke was too heavy to see Randi. Luke wouldn't abandon her. He dropped to the ground and felt around, trying to recall exactly where he had dropped her when he moved to break the window. His hands swept out in a wide circle. When his left hand bumped against her, he nearly yelled out his exaltation. He'd found her!

Grasping on to Randi with both hands, he dragged her inch by painful inch to the window. With each step he took, he grew more and more certain that he was too late. When he felt for her pulse, he was unsurprised when he couldn't find one.

He still refused to leave her behind. He wasn't sure whether it was the smoke or if she'd been more seriously wounded by her brother than they had suspected. If he didn't bring her body out, the truth would never be known. He owed it to her.

Lifting her body in his arms, he leaned over the rug-covered window and gently let her drop to the snow. He heard a soft cry from Jennie.

Looking back, he saw a wall of flame creeping closer. It was less than a foot away from him. Climbing up over the ledge, he braced his hand on the sill. A shard that wasn't covered by the rug pierced his skin. He flinched and jerked his hand away.

The heat from behind him singed his hair. He was out of time. He dove over the sill, tucking and rolling as he landed in the cold snow.

He lay still for a second before forcing himself to move.

Behind him, the destroyed Christmas tree was engulfed in flames. Two more seconds and he'd have been toast.

They weren't out of danger yet. The heat from the fire washed over his back. They needed to get farther away.

"Jennie! Help me move Randi away from the *haus*."

Jennie ran to him and grabbed hold of her friend. Her mouth trembled when she saw Randi's lifeless face. Her mouth trembled, but she assisted him without a word. They dragged Randi away from the burning structure. LJ waited for them near the tree. Jennie had tears running silently down her face. Luke tried not to look at her as she grieved for her friend.

"You should call the fire department," he said to her.

"I already did."

No sooner had she said that than they heard the wail of sirens. A large fire truck zoomed up the road, followed closely by a pickup truck with red flashing lights on the roof. When the pickup stopped, the driver got out and set a white helmet on his head, identifying him as the fire chief.

They were checked out by the paramedics. Trooper Carter arrived.

"Did you call him, too?" Luke whispered to Jennie.

She kept her gaze trained on the trooper as he talked with the fire chief. "I did. After everything that's happened, I figured he'd be more willing to buy that we were trapped in a burning house."

A few minutes later, Trooper Carter and the fire chief approached them. "According to my notes, this house belongs to a Miss Miranda Griggs, aged twenty-six."

Standing beside her, Luke heard Jennie gulp before she answered. "Yes, sir. That's her, over there."

Their gazes followed her pointing finger. There was a moment's silence while the two men stared at the body.

"I take it you knew her," the chief asked, his voice gentle.

Jennie bobbed her head once. "We went through the foster care system together. She was my best friend." There was a definite sob in her voice.

Luke edged closer so his arm was touching hers. She didn't acknowledge him, but her voice was stronger when she continued. "She asked me to come over. We heard something in the garage. Luke went to check it out, and the rest of us waited in the hall. The fire started so suddenly, I didn't see what happened."

"I know what caused it," Luke said. "There was a man in the garage. When I opened the door, he was pouring gas on a pile of firewood. He threw the can in the *haus*, then threw a flare in after it."

The chief rubbed his chin. "I noticed that the front door had been bolted shut."

Jennie's eyes widened. "That must have happened before we arrived. I never noticed that. I thought it was just locked."

"He never meant for anyone to get out of the house, which makes this first degree murder," Trooper Carter said. "It was a very careful job. Obviously planned out. Do either of you have any idea who would have done this?"

They both nodded. Luke responded, "It was Morgan, Randi's half brother. When we arrived, she was lying on the floor. He'd beaten her."

Jennie explained to Trooper Carter what Randi had found. "Is she—" She broke off.

Luke grabbed her hand. Regardless of having dragged Randi's limp body across the yard, Jennie was still hoping her friend was merely unconscious.

"I'm afraid so." Trooper Carter's normally flat expression brimmed with sympathy. "I'm sorry for your loss. We'll put out a bulletin on Morgan."

Luke opened his mouth to speak. He wanted to ask what they should do next. His words were cut off by a fit of coughing. His ears began to buzz. He couldn't breathe and the air in front of him seemed to shimmer, as if someone had tossed a handful of glitter in the air in front of him.

He put out an arm to reach for Jennie. Her face swam before his eyes.

He went down.

Jennie shrieked as Luke collapsed. All she could think about was that he was dead, too. She'd already lost him once. Even though she didn't really know him anymore, he was still Luke, the man she'd loved with her whole being.

"Luke!" Dropping to her knees in the snow beside him, she frantically searched for a pulse.

"Easy, miss." A paramedic nudged her aside to kneel next to Luke. "He's probably inhaled too much smoke. We need to get him to the hospital."

In shock, she watched as the paramedics swarmed about, getting him hooked up to oxygen and lifting him onto a stretcher. When the ambulance door slammed shut behind him, the sense of loss was a physical pain, a sharp invisible spear in her gut.

"Mama, Mama." LJ yanked on her hand, his little face frightened and tear streaked. "Where's Daddy going, Mama? Why wouldn't he wake up?"

Trooper Carter's face became grave. She was grateful when he didn't ask questions. Her emotions were too shaky to deal with complex explanations right now. All she wanted was to make sure that Luke would be all right.

It was strange how used to having him around she was getting after one day in his presence. Luke Beiler was not the same man she'd married, but she was already certain he was a man she could rely on. What she couldn't trust was the way she was drawn to him.

He had made the choice to become Amish, whether he'd had all the facts or not. There was nothing she could do to change that. Which meant it was irrelevant how wonderful or trustworthy he was, or how his smile made her pulse race. None of that was important.

As soon as this ended, if they were all still alive, he'd return to his Amish home with his Plain community. She and LJ would stay here. If she weren't careful, they'd both wind up with their hearts broken. She didn't want that for her son.

Nor did she see how she could stop him from getting to know his father.

It was his right. And it was Luke's right to know his son. She had seen how devastated he was to learn he'd missed seeing LJ grow.

She couldn't deny him the joy of seeing LJ become a man.

But how to do that without herself becoming emotionally dependent on him, she didn't know.

Ugh! This was becoming too complicated.

"Mrs. Beiler," Trooper Carter said as he approached her again. "I can give you a lift to the hospital if you want to check on your husband."

Jennie shook her head. "Thank you, but I have my car. I'll follow you."

LJ was disappointed. "I want to ride in the police car."

Trooper Carter lowered himself to his level. "You want to ride with me? Maybe I can have someone else drive your mom's car—how does that sound?"

She sighed. There was no way she could say no. Sure

enough, the little boy's eyes widened and a grin spread across his adorable face.

"Will you turn on the lights? And the siren?" LJ stared up at the trooper, his eyes pleading.

Trooper Carter chuckled. "I guess I can do that."

She cringed but managed a weak smile for her son. The last thing she wanted was to be seen sitting in a police car with sirens blaring and lights flashing. However, there was much to be said for the relief at seeing her son smiling, especially after the harrowing day they had had up to this point.

A quick glance over her shoulder told her that Randi's body had already been moved.

"We'll find him," Carter murmured.

She thanked him, then followed him to the police cruiser. At the car, his partner stood, waiting.

"Hey, Jill," Trooper Carter greeted the woman. "How would you like to drive a civilian car for a change, while I give my pal LJ here a fancy ride in our cruiser?"

Jill rolled her eyes. "Fine. Fine. Can I have the keys, please?"

Jennie dropped the keys into her open palm.

The entire way to the hospital, LJ chattered at the trooper, questions pouring from him at lightning speed. Jennie soon gave up trying to listen to the conversation. Her thoughts were too consumed with Luke's situation. Surely, if he had died, or if his condition had worsened, someone would have contacted Trooper Carter, wouldn't they? She hoped that was the case, but never having been in this situation, was unsure what to expect when they arrived.

Before she exited the vehicle, Trooper Carter stopped her. "I had a purpose for wanting to drive you. I didn't want any other ears to hear this, but whatever happens, I want you to promise me that you won't go back to your apartment. This is too coincidental, and I don't like it. Morgan. Steve. Too many variables. You need to disappear. Though, keep in contact."

The two directives seemed contradictory, but she nodded her head. "I get it. And we plan to do just that. As soon as we can collect Luke to go with us. We're still set to head to his uncle's house. It's outside of Meadville, halfway to Spartansburg. Most of the houses belong to Amish families. It's a very rural area. Highly unlikely anyone would think to look for us there. Especially since most of the people I see on a daily basis have no idea who Luke is or where he's from."

In the emergency room, their way was barred by a nurse. "Family only."

Jennie took a deep breath. "We are family. I'm his wife, and this is his son."

"I want to see my daddy." LJ went into full pout mode, his lower lip protruding, his bright blue eyes narrowing to slits as he glared at the nurse.

"It's okay, honey," Jennie murmured.

The nurse gave her a doubting expression.

"It's a long story, but he really is my husband."

With the support of the state trooper at Jennie's side, the nurse gave in, although not gracefully. Jennie and LJ were allowed back in the examination room.

To her relief, Luke was alive, though he didn't look happy.

"Jennie! LJ!" he exclaimed when they entered his curtained cubicle. "*Ach*, I was getting worried."

LJ clambered up to sit on the edge of the thin mattress with Luke. Jennie stepped close, but was careful not to get too close, remembering her resolution to keep her emotional distance.

Luke gave her a questioning glance. She ignored it. "I've never seen anyone hit the ground so fast. Are you okay?" she asked him.

His cheeks and the tips of his ears reddened. "*Jah*, I'm *gut*. I woke up on the ambulance. Breathed in too much smoke." He hesitated. The indecision on his face told her he was trying to decide if he should say something.

"They're out searching for Morgan," Jennie commented. "Trooper Carter came in with me. He all but ordered me to go off the grid until Steve or Morgan or anyone else gunning for me is found."

His brow raised. "Off the grid?"

"You know, hide. No cell phones, leave no trace, that sort of thing."

"*Jah*, I know what it means. Did you remind him we're heading to my *onkel* Jed's *haus*? You can't get more off the grid than an Amish community."

She snorted in reply, suppressing the odd desire to laugh. It seemed somehow wrong to laugh at a time like this. "Yeah, yeah. I told him. When can you leave?"

"Hopefully soon."

Soon turned out to be three hours later. Luke was examined and the cops came and went, taking with them his vague description of the man who set the fire. It was late afternoon before he was released from the hospital.

The parking lot was coated with a fresh layer of soft white snow. It was fluffy and pretty. And as slick as stepping on a sheet of ice. They walked with careful steps to the car. Still, Jennie's right leg shot out from underneath her when she hit a particularly icy patch. Luke caught her, wobbling as the force of her weight hitting his nearly took them both down.

The momentary contact rocked her as his warm breath washed over her face. It smelled like mint.

Why was she noticing this?

Flushing, she pushed away as soon as she could stand without embarrassing herself.

Exhausted, but alive, the three made it to her car.

"Mama, I'm hungry." LJ's whine broke into the somber silence that covered them like a thick fog.

"Okay, honey, we'll find something to eat."

Chicken nuggets and fries at a drive-thru turned out to be the best she could come up with at the moment.

"Your uncle, I know he lives off Route 77. I don't recall the road I turn on, though." She turned off the main street and headed up the hill, past a Kwik Fill gas station and away from Meadville.

"You've still got another fifteen or twenty minutes before you come to it," Luke said. "It's about five minutes after the turn off to Centerville."

"Got it."

She turned on the radio for some music, but then turned it off again when the news came on. She really didn't want to hear about the fire. She'd have nightmares for the rest of her life about Randi's death.

"I wonder," she began, then stopped.

"What?"

Jennie released a sigh. "I wonder if I'd seen Randi's call when she first tried to get a hold of me yesterday if she would still be alive now."

Luke placed his hand over hers. "Jennie, you can't do that to yourself. It's not right that she died. But there is nothing you can do to change it. Morgan is responsible for what happened, not you."

"I know that. In my mind. But I'm not sure I believe it."

EIGHT

It had never bothered him that he didn't have more charisma. Luke had never been a smooth talker, able to glibly know the right thing to say at any given time. That had never been his gift. Raymond, now, Raymond had always been far more eloquent. Which had never bothered Luke before.

Until now.

If only he knew the words to wipe the sorrow from Jennie's deep brown eyes. He wanted more than he could say to see the gold specks in her eyes shine. To see the way her left cheek dimpled when she smiled, truly smiled with her whole heart. In those moments, she was radiant.

He didn't even question how he knew that he used to enjoy basking in the glow of her happiness. He had no specific memories, but he knew it to be true.

Now he could do nothing. Nothing but hold her hand as the sorrow emanated from her like a strong perfume.

He was in a very dangerous position. For the foreseeable future, he was going to be sequestered with Jennie and LJ. While getting to know his son was a wonderful opportunity, and one that he would be forever grateful for, being in such close proximity to the woman he had once married was not a good idea.

Already his emotions were becoming far too tangled up where she was concerned. The mere sound of her voice soothed him in a way he would not have believed possible. Sitting so close beside her in the car, he could catch the whiff of the vanilla scent she wore. It was a scent that reminded him of home and all that was beautiful.

It was almost like a memory. Being so near her, he wondered if he closed his eyes and breathed in deep, would a memory spark of his life with her, that life he had lost?

It was useless to encourage such imaginings. He had made his choice when he had joined the Amish church, and he didn't regret it. It meant that *Gott* was the center of his world, and that's how he felt it should be. The problem was Jennie was no longer part of his future.

If only his heart could remember that.

He sneaked a peek at her face. It was more closed off than it had been earlier. When she had entered his cubicle in the emergency room, he had noticed that she seemed more reserved. It reminded him of the moment when he had met her again in her apartment. It was hard to believe that was only yesterday.

He found himself wishing for the closeness that had started to grow between them. But that would only lead to more pain and heartache when they had to part again. Would he still be able to keep in touch with his son when this was over?

Beside him, Jennie flicked on the blinker. They were turning onto his *onkel* Jed's road. Luke sat straighter in his seat.

"*Gut*, go down the road. *Onkel* Jed's farm is almost two miles down."

"All right. I've never been to his actual house. When I worked with you guys on the housing mission, we always met at a church near Union City."

"I remember that church. I haven't been there in years."

"Really?" She slowed at a particularly slippery spot. "I would have thought that you would have been very involved in the mission. Building houses was kind of your passion back then."

Building *hauser* was his passion.

"I remember that," he said slowly. A memory of sitting on a roof with Jennie bloomed in his mind. "I don't know what happened. When I returned to my parents' *haus*, I started helping my *daed* in his carpentry shop. I don't build *hauser* but I do build furniture."

She pursed her lips together. He could almost hear the words she was holding back behind those tightly clamped lips.

"It's not the same, ain't so?" he mused. "You're right."

"I didn't say a word."

He grinned at her prim voice. "*Nee*, you didn't have to. Your face said it just fine." He sighed. "That's the *haus*."

"The white one?"

He laughed. All the *hauser* on the block were white. "Amish homes are almost always white. No one's *haus* stands out. We are all equal, and our homes and the way we dress proclaims that."

"I wasn't making fun."

"*Jah*. This I know. Let's go see if *Onkel* Jed and *Tante* Eleanor are home."

Jennie started to slow down. They were almost to the driveway when she glanced up in the mirror and frowned.

"Hey!" Luke watched as she drove right past the place. "You missed the drive."

"I didn't miss it," she growled, her voice sliding out between clenched teeth. "Someone is following us. I'm not sure if it's one of Steve's friends or not."

Luke swiveled around in his seat to see the car behind them. The glare of the sun bouncing off the windshield made it impossible to see who was driving. It might have been Morgan, it might have been Steve, it might have been someone totally unrelated to what had been happening for the past two days. Although that seemed highly unlikely.

Apparently, Jennie wasn't willing to take the chance, and Luke couldn't find a single fault with that. The car hit a bump, and his head hit the ceiling. He sank back down in his seat, rubbing his head.

"You okay back there, LJ?" he asked.

"Fine, Daddy!" LJ sang back, completely oblivious to the terror stirring in both of his parents. Luke gave him what he hoped was a smile, but strongly suspected it was more of a grimace.

"That's a dark blue sedan," he remarked to Jennie in a low voice. "It looks like the same car that almost ran you over yesterday. Or at least, I think it does. I can't be sure. Can we go any faster? Do you think we can lose them?"

Jennie bit her lip and glanced into the mirror again. "I don't want to risk spinning out on this road. If we lose control, we'd be completely vulnerable."

"Okay. Let's do our best to lose him without skidding into a ditch, then."

"Hold on." Jennie's face was grim as she leaned into the steering wheel, digging in to drive them to safety. Luke reached up and grabbed the handle near the top of the door, praying with all his might for their safety and that *Gott* would bring them out of this mess. Alive.

Jennie maneuvered the car to the next intersection, slowing down in order to look up the hill to her left to see if there was any oncoming traffic.

SLAM!

Her head whipped forward and banged against the steering wheel. She slid out onto the road. LJ cried out. A quick glance back assured her that he was uninjured. The car that hit them spun sideways at the impact. Maybe they had a reprieve, time to get away.

A horn blew. An eighteen-wheeler was barreling down the hill, and Jennie's car was directly in its path. Shoving her foot down on the gas, she gunned the car forward, fishtailing on the icy road. The semi blew past her, horn blaring, its momentum sucking her car back for a second before she was able to move smoothly back into her lane.

She doubted it had been enough to deter the car that was chasing them. A quick glance in her mirror confirmed her fears.

"He's still behind us."

"Mama, I'm scared. I don't like this anymore!"

Her heart bled at the fear she heard in her son's voice.

"LJ." Luke turned and looked at their son. "I know this is scary. Your mama and I are both here."

She risked a quick look into the back seat to see tears dappling his chubby little cheeks.

"Maybe you could pray for us." Had that really just popped out of her mouth? Judging from the disbelief on Luke's face, it had. She winced. She'd never been one to turn to God. Asking for His help when she was in trouble seemed rather hypocritical.

"*Jah*, I can do that."

While Luke prayed with LJ, Jennie rounded another curve. The road straightened out and started to slope downward at an alarming angle. The snow was coming thicker now, falling in heavy white flakes that clumped on her windshield wipers. They were already swiping the glass at full speed and having trouble keeping up.

The wind was howling, blowing the onslaught of snow across the road in blustery drifts. She could no longer tell where the road was. Every few feet, she'd catch a glimpse of dirt, and then she'd see the deep ditch on the side of the road. If they landed in that, there would be no way out.

She had no choice but to slow down.

Tapping the brakes lightly, she cried out when she felt the car starting to veer out of control. "God, help me!"

It was the first prayer she'd uttered since she was fifteen years old, but she meant it with her whole being.

The car slid another few feet before it came back under her control. She peered into the mirror. The blue sedan picked up speed and followed them down the hill.

"He's moving too fast," Luke observed, his voice harsh. She'd never heard him so grim. "If he hits us, we'll both spin out of control."

"I don't know what to do." Jennie gently put more pressure on the gas. When the car started to move sideways, she backed off and tapped the brakes again. This time, when the car slid, it stayed on the road. "We can't go any faster than this and keep in control."

They were out of options.

There was a road off to the right. Deciding she didn't have any other choices, Jennie gripped the wheel and swerved onto the road. The vehicle dipped and bumped along as the back tire barely skimmed over the side of the ditch.

That was way too close.

This road was narrower than the one they'd just left. Tall, thick trees dotted the sides, close to the edge. If she went off the road now, she doubted she could do so without ramming into one of the trees.

Her tires skimmed over the myriad of potholes hidden by snow, the sound roaring in her ears.

"Is he still behind us?" she yelled out to Luke, not daring to take her eyes off the road.

He turned and looked back. "Still there." He pointed at a barn in the distance. "There's a side road just past that barn. It's easier to navigate. Maybe turn there."

It couldn't be any worse than the road they were on now. When she was almost to the barn, she saw it—it was one of those roads with no sign. It might not have made it on the map, but all the locals would recognize it.

She turned on the road, slowing as little as she could. The blue car kept pace with her. By now, Jennie was starting to despair of ever breaking free of him. What would he do if he caught up with them? She shuddered, attempting to force her mind away from the thought. She only prayed that if he did catch up with them, somehow LJ would be spared. She didn't hold out any such hope for herself or Luke.

Their pursuer might not understand the concept of mercy.

The blue car barreled closer. Just when Jennie feared it would hit them, it started to slide.

"He's losing control!" Her knuckles whitened as she gripped the wheel.

Looking in her mirror, she witnessed the exact moment when the blue car spun out, spiraling in two full circles before spinning across the road and going nose-first into a ditch.

"He's out." She flexed her fingers. Her hold on the steering wheel had been so tight, little darts of pain were shooting down her fingers.

"He's not getting out of that soon," Luke agreed. "I can't see the license plate number. When we get to *Onkel* Jed's, let's call Trooper Carter. He can send some-one out and we'll maybe know who was after us."

"Okay." She frowned. "I don't want to try to drive back up this hill. Without four-wheel drive, I doubt my car will be able to handle the hill. We don't need to join our friend in that ditch."

Luke nodded his agreement. "Let's take the long way around. What do you say?"

She smiled. "The scenic route it is."

Jennie followed Luke's directions, taking the curves and turns at a safe speed now that they weren't being followed. Her shoulders still twitched, feeling like someone would be coming after them at any second.

She had never wanted out of a vehicle so badly.

The light in the afternoon sky was growing dim by the time they finally made it to Jed Beiler's home. There were no electric lights in the house, but Jennie could see the house was still fairly illuminated.

"It's brighter than I expected an Amish home to be," she commented as she drove into the lane leading up to the house.

"*Jah. Onkel*'s bishop has allowed the use of natural gas to light the *hauser*. It can create plenty of light. *Onkel* has the lanterns built into his home, although some members in the community have rolling lights that can be moved from room to room."

"What do your parents use?" She wasn't just asking to talk. She was sincerely interested. It wasn't something she'd ever considered before.

"Neither." He unbuckled his seat belt as the car rolled to a stop. "The community my parents live in is very strict. They use kerosene lamps. Not as bright, but they serve their purpose."

She frowned. "Wouldn't that be more dangerous, having kerosene lamps through your house?"

"*Jah*. Maybe so. We learn to be careful."

She thought he was joking but there wasn't a hint of a smile on his face. Getting out of the car, she marveled at how different his life was now to how it was when they were together. It was hard to imagine him being okay with all the things he had once rejected, but it didn't seem to bother him anymore.

The fact that it didn't bothered her.

The front door opened, and a tall man stepped out on the porch. He leaned forward, peering into the dim light. "*Hallo?* Who is here? Are you lost?"

"*Onkel* Jed, it's Luke."

"*Ach*, Luke, come on in."

Jennie helped LJ out of the car. He resisted being carried, insisting on walking. She gave in, reminding herself to pick her battles wisely.

"Who do you have here?" Eleanor Beiler wiped her hands dry on a towel before joining them in the open family room.

The moment Jed stared Jennie in the face, recognition dawned. "Jennie Forster! I'd know you anywhere. I didn't know you two were still friends." She didn't miss the anxious glance he speared his nephew with. Apparently, Luke's family were all wary of the relationship that had developed between them.

She was so tired of it all. She slanted a glance at Luke, striving not to let it become a glare. She was not the enemy. She had no plans to lead him astray, and she was in danger.

Luke clearly tensed at the look his uncle and aunt exchanged. In fact, he looked irritated.

"*Onkel* Jed, *Tante* Eleanor, I'm glad you remember Jennie. It's Jennie Beiler now."

Jennie nearly fainted. She wouldn't have been surprised if his aunt and uncle had, as well.

"I didn't know it when I woke from my accident, but while I was away from New Wilmington, Jennie and I were married. She thought I was dead for the past five years."

Their eyes all widened. Then they zeroed in on LJ. Luke wasn't done. "LJ, come here."

LJ immediately went to his father.

"*Tante*, *Onkel*, this is Luke Junior. My son."

NINE

Luke would not allow himself to feel guilty for dropping that announcement in the middle of the room and watching it explode. The look his uncle had sent toward Jennie, as if she were somehow at fault for his troubles, infuriated him. No one had the right to judge her. No one. Not even his family.

"Your wife." *Tante* Eleanor's voice was a thin whisper cutting through the silence.

"*Jah.* My wife. She and LJ are in danger. We came here hoping to find a refuge where her life would be safe."

At the mention of danger, the atmosphere changed. Jed and Eleanor would good people. He'd never doubted that they would embrace Jennie and LJ once they were aware of the whole story.

"Danger!" Jed strode forward. "*Cumme! Cumme!* You look tired."

Luke put his hand on the small of Jennie's back. When she glanced at him, startled, he dropped his hand. He could not treat her as if she were his wife in truth. He had no reason to be touching her. He clenched his fist at his side and followed her into the kitchen area.

"4 for 4" MINI-SURVEY

We are prepared to **REWARD** you with 4 FREE Books and Free Gifts for completing our MINI SURVEY!

Romance

Suspense

You'll get up to...
4 FREE BOOKS & FREE GIFTS

st for participating in our Mini Survey!

Get Up To 4 Free Books!

Dear Reader,

IT'S A FACT: if you answer 4 quick
questions, we'll send you 4 FREE REWARDS
from each series you try!

Try **Love Inspired® Romance Larger-Print**
books and fall in love with inspirational
romances that take you on an uplifting journey
of faith, forgiveness and hope.

Try **Love Inspired® Suspense Larger-Print**
books where courage and optimism unite in
stories of faith and love in the face of danger.

Or **TRY BOTH!**

I'm not kidding you. As a leading publisher
of women's fiction, we value your opinions…
and your time. That's why we are prepared
to reward you handsomely for completing
our mini-survey. In fact, we have 4 Free
Rewards for you, including 2 free books and
2 free gifts from each series you try!

Thank you for participating in
our survey,

Pam Powers

www.ReaderService.com

To get your 4 FREE REWARDS:
Complete the survey below and return the insert today to receive up to 4 FREE BOOKS and FREE GIFTS guaranteed!

"4 for 4" MINI-SURVEY

1 Is reading one of your favorite hobbies?
☐ YES ☐ NO

2 Do you prefer to read instead of watch TV?
☐ YES ☐ NO

3 Do you read newspapers and magazines?
☐ YES ☐ NO

4 Do you enjoy trying new book series with FREE BOOKS?
☐ YES ☐ NO

Please send me my Free Rewards, consisting of **2 Free Books from each series I select** and **Free Mystery Gifts**. I understand that I am under no obligation to buy anything, as explained on the back of this card.
❏ **Love Inspired® Romance Larger-Print** (122/322 IDL GQ5X)
❏ **Love Inspired® Suspense Larger-Print** (107/307 IDL GQ5X)
❏ **Try Both** (122/322 & 107/307 IDL GQ6A)

FIRST NAME	LAST NAME

ADDRESS

APT.#	CITY

STATE/PROV.	ZIP/POSTAL CODE

EMAIL ❏ Please check this box if you would like to receive newsletters and promotional emails from Harlequin Enterprises ULC and its affiliates. You can unsubscribe anytime.

"Dinner won't be for an hour or so." Eleanor brought a pitcher of water to the table. "We can talk for a bit until the others are finished with their chores."

Luke loved his cousins, but he was relieved to know that he and Jennie would have some time alone to give his *tante* and *onkel* the main points of what was happening. The fewer people who knew the sordid tale, the better.

As expected, his relatives were full of sympathy for Jennie. Although, he did detect several concerned looks cast his way. Well, he wasn't backing out. He would help Jennie as long as he needed in order to ensure she and LJ were safe. It was the right thing to do.

He also couldn't bear the idea of returning home with no assurance that they were well. Whatever happened, for now, they were in his care. He would not fail them, no matter what it cost him.

Some of his determination must have shown when Jed met his eyes. The older man's gaze dropped, his shoulders sagging slightly, resignation stamped on his face.

LJ's lids began to droop before their conversation was over. Jennie pulled him into her arms. Luke couldn't keep his eyes off the beautiful sight of the mother cradling her child.

If only...

He blocked the thought. When the rest of the family arrived, all conversation about the danger that was hunting Jennie ceased. Eleanor and Jed introduced her as Luke's friend who'd be staying with them for a short time. His cousins accepted the information calmly.

Luke tried to suppress his annoyance at the way she was introduced. He wanted to be able to tell them that LJ was his. His uncle laid a stern eye on him. He nodded, understanding the warning, though he didn't like it.

When he went to bed that evening, he shared a room with one of his cousins. He lay awake in bed long after his cousin drifted off to sleep, reliving the moment when the gas had exploded in Randi's house. Regret filled him that he had been unable to save her. It wasn't his fault, he knew that. He had managed to get Jennie and LJ out, it was true, but he would never forget the memory of Randi's still body lying in the snow. It should never have happened.

None of this should be happening.

He squeezed his eyes tight, shying away from thoughts of what could have happened on the road earlier that day. It seemed everywhere they went, danger followed.

Inhaling deeply, Luke prayed for guidance. He prayed that *Gott* would continue to protect them and bring those who would cause harm to Jennie and LJ to justice.

He also prayed for help guarding his heart.

But he feared that prayer was too late.

The next morning, he awoke early to find his cousin had already left. *Ach.* Luke should have risen to help with the morning chores. Dressing quickly, he left the *haus* to go find his cousins and *onkel*.

The day passed in an uneventful manner, for which he was grateful. It didn't stop him from looking over his shoulders, waiting for someone to take a shot at them or to attempt to run them over.

At least they went to bed that night with no additional injuries. That was a blessing, for sure.

* * *

On Sunday, no chores were done. Luke and Jennie took advantage of the time to get rested up. When he'd mentioned that Trooper Carter had told Jennie to go off the grid and hide, his *tante* had suggested that while they were here, Jennie dress in his cousin's dresses. He supposed she thought that Jennie would blend in more and not be so easy for her attackers to find.

It made sense. The problem, as far as he was concerned, was that it was harder to remember why Jennie was off-limits to him when she looked like a lovely Plain woman. His cousin's pink dress and crisp white *kapp*, in his mind, enhanced Jennie's natural beauty. She used to wear cosmetics, and she'd been beautiful. But he thought she was breathtaking now without any additional products.

Monday morning dawned clear, though Luke had an ache in his leg that he knew from experience meant it would snow later. Somehow, he always knew. The doctor told him that he might be more sensitive to changes in barometric pressure. So far, the doctor had been correct.

Luke was given the chore of chopping more firewood. His relatives used it for their own *haus*, but they also sold wood to the surrounding area. "It's *gut* business and it helps our friends."

Luke liked the manual labor. As he worked, the motion of chopping the wood brought back an image of working on a *haus* with his *onkel*. He paused briefly, willing the image to become focused.

And then he saw it clearly. He heard a laugh. It was a younger Jennie. His mind recalled that day, eight years earlier, when they had finished the first *haus* they had worked on. Jennie had been painting, and he had worked on the roof. When they were finished, he'd taken her out to a restaurant to eat. And later that night, before he'd left, he'd kissed her.

His eyes flared open wide, his pulse thumping through his veins.

"Hey, Luke."

For a second, he thought the voice was part of his memory. When he heard it again, he turned to find Jennie standing several feet away, her head tilted to the side as she considered him with concern. "You okay?"

"Jah." He swallowed, shoving the memory aside. "I'm *gut.* Just thinking."

He wasn't about to tell her that he'd been thinking about her. Or that he'd been remembering their first kiss. The tips of his ears warmed, but he strove to retain a facade of nonchalance.

She waited. When he said nothing more, she shrugged and let the matter drop as he had hoped she would. "Your uncle has some errands he wondered if we'd run for him."

Luke frowned. "I'm not sure—do you think it's safe?"

She chewed on her lip. "Well, if he had asked us to drive into town, I'd say no. As it is, all he's asked is that we walk to the Amish store and pick up some baking items for your aunt. I'll admit, I wouldn't mind the trip, but I don't want to go by myself."

He thought about it. They would be staying in the Amish area. They could even cut through the back paths. After a moment he nodded. "I think we could do that. Give me a moment to put this ax back in the barn."

As he walked past, she dropped in beside him. He

clasped his hands behind his back to avoid the temptation of reaching out and grabbing hold of her hand. When she tucked her own hands beneath her black cape, he wondered if she was fighting the same temptation.

Then he scolded himself for wishing it was true.

A squeal of tires on the street had them both whirling to face the road. A car thundered past, stopping in front. Luke threw his body in front of Jennie as the driver pointed a gun in their direction.

"Get down!" Pushing her down against the barn, Luke covered her body with his as the gunner opened fire.

Debris rained down around them as a bullet hit the barn, leaving a fist-size hole in the wood. A second shot hit just inches away from Jennie's head. She couldn't breathe, feeling the wood exploding around her.

As scared as she was for herself, she was terrified for Luke, hovering over her. She didn't want to save her life at the cost of his. Even as she tried to push him away so he could get lower, he moved off her, groaning.

The car raced away.

Blood was streaming from a wound in Luke's shoulder. A large chunk of wood, debris from the garage, had impaled him straight through his coat.

"Luke!" she screamed.

"*Ach*, don't worry so, Jennie girl," he said, smiling at her, his eyes lined with pain. "It's nothing. Just a large splinter. Far better than a bullet, ain't so?"

"Luke, don't joke. You're hurt." She could barely choke out the words.

"It's not so bad. I'm alive, and so are you."

She agreed, struggling to remain calm.

Within seconds, he was surrounded by family and friends. She stepped back to allow them room, but his lids snapped open again. He searched frantically among the host of people surrounding him, prodding and asking questions, until he found her.

"Jennie."

She stepped closer. He sat up and his coat flapped open. Underneath, his shirt was covered with blood, but it didn't seem to be spreading.

"Where's LJ?"

"The child's taking a nap," Luke's aunt assured him. He didn't seem to hear her.

"Check on him, please?"

Jennie caught some of his urgency. "I will."

Pausing only long enough to be sure Luke was okay, she flew back into the house and up the stairs. LJ had been placed in the room at the end of the hall. His door was shut. Jennie ran to the door and opened it.

Her heart stopped. The window was wide open, the cold air rushing in. LJ was nowhere in sight.

Her baby had been kidnapped.

Taking the stairs two at a time, she leaped down the last three and rushed outside, shouting as she went. "Luke! Luke! LJ's gone! LJ's been taken!"

Luke shot up from where his aunt had been tending him, ignoring his bleeding shoulder. "Are you sure?"

She nodded, tears streaming down her cheeks. "The window was open and he was gone. The door to the room was still closed." She gulped, unable to manage any more.

Luke took over. "*Onkel*, there had to have been two of them. The one in the car shot at me. There's no way he could have gotten to LJ without us noticing. His partner was probably on foot. He must have gone through the back pastures."

"We'll search for him. Jennie, go into my office and call for your police."

Jennie didn't hesitate. She took off and went into the office. She dialed with shaking fingers.

"911. What's your emergency?"

"Someone has taken my son. He's only four." She choked on a sob. *Hold it together, Jennie. LJ needs you to be strong.*

"Ma'am, can you verify your location?"

Stumbling a bit over the address, she gave the dispatcher the information, as well as LJ's appearance and what he'd been dressed in.

"A police car has been dispatched from Union City, ma'am. They should be at your address within ten minutes. Can you stay on the line until they arrive?"

She didn't want to. "My son. I should be looking for my son."

"Ma'am, you need to stay on the line. If we need any more information, you're our contact."

Impatience and anxiety vibrated in her blood as she waited. Ten minutes had never seemed to take so long. What was Luke's family doing now? Was Luke searching? Of course he was. Luke would do anything for LJ. If the kidnapper was nearby, Luke would search until he found his son.

If she'd had her phone on her, she could have walked outside and seen what was happening. Unfortunately, she'd shut her phone off and left it in her room to save the battery. Plus, the Amish dress she was wearing had no pockets.

She slammed the phone down when the police pulled

in, running to meet the troopers before they had completely stopped the car. "My son is missing. Someone took him."

She could see the look in their eyes. They thought she was being melodramatic. "Call Trooper Carter with the state police if you don't believe me. Tell him LJ Beiler is missing. This is the second kidnapping attempt in four days. He'll tell you."

The condescending smiles disappeared. One of the troopers immediately got on his phone; the other had her repeat the details she'd already told the dispatcher.

The troopers joined in the search, one on foot while the other drove off to search the surrounding area in his cruiser. Jennie was told to remain near the house in case LJ came home. She was given explicit instructions to call the police if he returned.

A minute later, she was alone in a mother's worst nightmare.

TEN

Luke trudged through the snow, ignoring the wet flakes pelting his cheeks as he searched for his son. LJ had been missing for twenty minutes. Every minute he was gone, Luke's sense of desperation grew.

Around him, he could hear the other men searching, including the police trooper that had joined them on foot. They'd all spread out to cover more area. Luke veered to the right, taking the path that would lead him behind the lumberyard. The path was rocky, and he stumbled more than once over tree roots and debris. His shoulder still ached from being impaled with the wood from the barn.

He wouldn't let himself be distracted by the injury.

Part of him worried about what would happen if he found the man. Luke had no weapon, and his Amish beliefs forbade him from using a weapon, even if he had one at his disposal. Not that he wanted to. Luke had flouted a few rules in the past few days in his quest to keep Jennie and LJ alive, but he would not take a life. Not even to save his own.

He would, however, willingly put himself in harm's way to protect those he cared about.

Like he had earlier when he and Jennie were being shot at.

A flash of color to the left caught his attention. It was a bold color. Red. Like a scarf. It was moving. Walking as quietly as he could, he followed who or what was moving around in the woods.

After a few minutes, he was rewarded with a low whimper. LJ. His son was ahead. Scared, possibly hurt, but alive. Sending up a silent prayer of thanks and a plea for guidance, Luke kept moving closer.

"Quit your whining, kid," a man's voice growled.

LJ stopped whimpering. Since there was no other sound, Luke doubted the boy had been harmed. He needed to stay focused if he were to get to his son and bring the boy home to his mother.

Five minutes later, his prayers were answered. He saw his son being hauled over the shoulder of his kidnapper. A man that Luke had seen once before when he'd set his own sister's house on fire with her inside it.

Morgan Griggs had Luke's son.

Briefly, Luke wondered who'd driven the car. Was it Steve Curtis? He doubted it. Trooper Carter had Curtis's picture all over. While Luke didn't have access to a computer, he knew that in the *Englisch* world, most people walked around connected to the internet with their tablets or their smartphones. Even Jennie normally carried a phone with her.

There was no way Curtis could come here undisguised and not be recognized by someone.

Morgan was slowing down. He pulled his phone from his pocket but seemed to have trouble using it with one hand. Luke tensed as the man grabbed hold of LJ with both hands. When Morgan set the child on the ground,

Luke edged closer, careful to stay concealed behind the trees.

"Don't move," Morgan barked. "I mean it."

LJ didn't move, his little body trembling as he stared up at the man, eyes bulging and fearful.

Morgan dialed a number. "Where are you located? Yeah, I think that Amish store is somewhere up ahead. I can meet you there."

Luke edged closer. When a twig snapped under his foot, he halted. Morgan didn't react. "I heard the Amber Alert, so you know the place has to be crawling with cops... How should I know? It was your idea to lure her away by stealing the kid. I know he wants us to bring her."

Morgan hung up the phone. Luke needed to act now.

With a roar, he raced into the clearing, putting himself between Morgan and LJ. Morgan leaped toward him. Luke was waiting. He took the other man's weight and pulled him down.

Morgan, however, had more experience as a fighter. He managed to squirm out of Luke's hold. He might have gone for LJ again, but running feet were crashing through the woods. Luke's yell had brought the others running.

With a hateful glare at Luke, Morgan sprinted away.

LJ launched himself into his father's arms. Luke knelt on the ground, holding his son close to him, not knowing who was shaking more.

"Luke, ist er gut?" Onkel Jed demanded, racing up beside them. The older man dropped to his knees beside them, breathing heavily.

"Jah, er ist gut," he responded, telling his *onkel* that LJ was fine.

More shuffling sounds heralded the arrival of others. The police trooper shouldered his way to the front of the line. "How did you locate him? Is he hurt?"

Luke stood, LJ in his arms. "*Nee*, he is *gut*. He was taken by a man named Morgan Griggs. Griggs murdered his sister Friday by burning her *haus* down."

The Amish men all muttered, appalled at this news.

"He stopped here to make a phone call," Luke explained. "The person who shot at us earlier was supposed to meet him—"

"Hold on!" the police trooper interrupted. "You were shot at?"

Luke rapidly took him through the morning's events, making sure to describe the car. He also mentioned that he believed it was the same car that had tried to run him and Jennie off the road several days ago. The moment he finished talking, the trooper moved away, calling his partner with the news.

Luke wanted to get LJ back to the *haus* so he could get the child warm and assure his *mamm* that he was well. Jennie must be going out of her mind with worry. Luke's shoulder ached, and his leg was hurting something fierce, but he wasn't ready to set LJ back down. LJ didn't seem ready, either. The child clung to him, his face pressed against Luke's neck.

The moment they appeared in the yard, Jennie was there, running out to meet them.

"Mama! Mama!" LJ wriggled to get free.

Luke set him down and watched the reunion between mother and child.

"Where did you find him?" Jennie asked.

He found it hard to speak for a moment as her luminous gaze told him he was her hero. He cleared his throat. "Morgan had him."

"How—"

He shook his head. "I'll tell you what happened. Let's get him in the *haus*. He's been out in the cold too long."

LJ wasn't willing to walk, so Luke helped Jennie navigate the icy drive and the steps of the front porch. Once she was inside, Luke had to force himself to remove his arm from around her. He could still feel her warmth after she moved away from him.

It didn't surprise either Luke or Jennie when Trooper Carter showed up later that evening.

"We've done a full check on Morgan Griggs. We've also looked into his sister. It might interest you to know that Randi owned a blue Honda Accord." He showed them a picture of the make and model.

"That looks like the car we saw," Jennie confirmed. "It must be fairly new. The last time we got together she had a red CRV."

Carter nodded as if he expected that answer. "I figured. It seemed odd that you wouldn't know what car your best friend drove. Anyway, Randi reported her car stolen last week. My guess is her brother was the thief."

"Well, Morgan wasn't driving it today."

"Jah." Luke spoke up. "He was on foot and meeting up with someone else."

"So we have at least two people who are after you."

"Three," Luke said. Jennie and Trooper Carter both looked at him. "When Morgan was talking on the phone, he specifically told the person on the line that 'he wants her brought to him.' There has to be another person."

Next to him, Jennie seemed to deflate. "He must

have meant Steve. I don't think I'll ever be free of that man."

"Is there anyone else you know, anyone you can think of who might have been in league with Steve and Morgan? Anyone at all?"

"I don't know that many people that well," she said slowly. She went over who had she seen in the past week. "One person who might be upset with me is Pete Walsh. He's a guy I know who always made me uneasy."

Trooper Carter wrote the name down. "We'll look into him."

"What about that Deets person?" Luke asked suddenly. "The man who was taking pictures of LJ at school?"

Tante Eleanor gasped behind them.

Trooper Carter nodded. "Still looking for him." His phone rang. He excused himself to take the call.

Jennie let her shoulders droop. "I don't know how much more of this I can take before I lose it."

Tante Eleanor walked over to the table. "*Gott* is there for you, Jennie. He will be your help in these difficult times. If you let Him."

Jennie's brown eyes were troubled. "I've ignored God for so long, blaming Him for not helping when I needed it most. Will He still hear me?"

Her face filled with compassion, the older woman laid her hand on Jennie's shoulder. "We all fail at times. It's our nature, *jah*? *Gott* is always there. You can trust Him."

Jennie was so tired of fighting on her own. The idea that God really had stuck with her was incredible. She was just too worn out to work it out now. But maybe she didn't need to work it out for herself. Eleanor had said all she needed to do was trust.

Could it be that simple?

Not easy. Trusting someone else, even God, wasn't easy for Jennie. She'd been taking care of her own problems for too long for it to be easy to trust anyone else to help her.

God, if You're still there for me, if it's not too late, I want to believe. I'm in a bind and I could use some help.

Jennie sat there as peace flooded her vulnerable soul. She was overwhelmed. There was no lightning or sky-writing. In the grand scheme of things, her situation was not altered to any extent. Yet, she was different, knowing that to God, she mattered.

"Jennie?"

She realized that Luke and Eleanor were watching her with wary eyes. LJ had fallen asleep, leaning against her side. She hugged him close, then turned to respond to the unasked questions reflected in the faces surrounding her.

"I'm fine, Luke." How did she explain the profound change she'd just gone through? Metaphorically speaking, God had just released her from the cocoon her self-imposed isolation had placed her in. "I can't really explain it. I sat here, at your aunt's table, feeling more helpless than I've felt in a long time."

He made a noise. She waved his concern away.

"It's okay. Really. I prayed, truly prayed, like I've never done. I can't even remember the words I said, only that it was from the heart. Now…"

"You're at peace," he finished for her.

Their gazes connected. The air hummed between them. "Exactly."

Tante Eleanor frowned as her eyes ping-ponged between them. "*Jah.* That's what happens when you reach out to *Gott.* He is bigger than our problems."

Jennie nodded. Her arm was falling asleep where LJ was leaning against it, but she wasn't ready to put him to bed. She wasn't going to let him out of her sight anytime in the near future.

Trooper Carter returned. "The car hasn't been located yet, although there's been a possible sighting. It's being checked out." He promised to let them know if they found either Morgan Griggs or the car. "There's still a widespread search for Steve Curtis through the Commonwealth of Pennsylvania. There've been three sightings near Philadelphia. None of them have panned out into anything useful at this point. If he is that far away, it puts some doubt on the theory that he's behind your troubles."

"Who else could be behind it?" Jennie drummed her fingers on the table. Did no one see how odd it was that her attacks coincided with his escape?

Trooper Carter raised his hands. "I know. It probably is him. I believe it is, but at this point, the evidence trail is rather thin."

"You can connect him and Morgan," she argued.

"We can put them both in the same prison, yes." He shook his head as she opened her mouth. "The guards have been questioned. Curtis and Griggs were rarely in each other's company, that they can recall. If they had been planning something, it was very discreet. Look, Jennie, I'll keep searching. Maybe it does all lead back to him. All I'm saying is we have little to go on."

Soon after delivering that disappointing news, Trooper Carter departed, promising to keep her informed. Luke took LJ and laid him on the couch in the front room.

"He'll be more comfortable, and we'll be able to see him."

She nodded but didn't respond, anger still churning and bubbling. "I don't think I can stay here any longer," she blurted.

Luke plopped down on the bench across from her, his eyes going flat at her announcement.

"Where would you go?"

"I don't know." She dropped her head in her hands as the impossibility of it all washed over her.

"If you leave, I'm going with you."

Startled, she raised her head to stare at the man watching her. He was the Luke she remembered, but not. Her Luke had been so easygoing, almost carefree. She recalled being irritated at times in their marriage by his lack of decisiveness. This older, more mature version was resolute. The carefree youth had been obliterated by life.

She found herself approving of the changes she witnessed. Even though some of those changes were creating a wedge between them ever having a real future together.

She had turned to God. But she was still not part of Luke's world. That would never change.

Or could it?

She turned away from the question. It was impossible to think through now. Nor did it matter when lives, namely hers and LJ's, were at stake.

"I'm serious, Jennie. If you want to leave, we'll leave together. Find somewhere else to hide."

The smile that started in her heart seeped onto her

face. Just a little. She didn't want him to know how relieved she was. Until he insisted, she hadn't realized that she had expected him to join her. Doing this without him was not something she wanted to consider.

"Where would you go?" Eleanor set a loaf of freshly baked cinnamon rolls in the center of the table, gesturing that they should help themselves. She went to the stove and lifted the coffeepot she'd set there to brew. Jennie watched as she efficiently gathered mugs and set them on a plain serving tray.

When she set it on the table, Jennie murmured her thanks and reached out a hand for a roll. They were warm, soft and sticky. Her mouth was watering before her teeth sank into the first delicious bite.

"I haven't thought that far ahead." Jennie hated not having a plan. "I don't know that many people that I trust or that would have the capability to shelter us. Only my brother, and he won't be home until the day after Christmas."

That was still four days away. A new thought occurred to her. Trooper Carter had previously said that Steve might search for her at Aiden's house. She didn't want to bring trouble to her brother's family. Nor could she stay here.

"I know." Luke spoke around a mouthful of cinnamon roll. His aunt smacked his shoulder lightly. He ducked his head and swallowed like a kid. Jennie bit back a smile.

"What do you know?" Jennie asked.

He washed the roll down with a gulp of coffee. "I know where we can go. I don't know why I didn't think of it earlier."

She raised one eyebrow. "Well? Don't keep me in suspense. Where?"

"We'll go to my parents' *haus*. No one will think to look for you among the Amish communities in New Wilmington."

She raised his eyebrows at him. "They found me here."

He shrugged. "You thought we were being followed. Plus, you spent time with us here. People in the area know you. Someone could have identified you. But in New Wilmington, you'd be a stranger. There are nearly twenty districts there. The Amish aren't ones to talk about their business to outsiders, so I don't think they'd have much chance of ferreting out your location."

Ferreting out? He might not remember his years as an *Englischer*, but there were moments when he sounded like one.

It wasn't a bad idea. They talked, making plans for how to make the journey.

"We could leave first thing in the morning," Luke remarked. "As soon as breakfast is done."

"New Wilmington is what? An hour and a half away?" Jennie asked.

"I think it would take us almost two hours to drive there."

Jennie had no appetite at dinner, but she tried to do justice to the delicious meal Eleanor served. Afterwards, she stayed to assist Luke's aunt to clean up. Luke stood near Jennie at the counter, finalizing plans.

"Luke," Jed said, wandering back into the kitchen. "That trooper that was here earlier just pulled in."

Trooper Carter was back? The knot that seemed

to perpetually sit in Jennie's belly immediately grew. The coffee she'd been drinking sat uncomfortably in her gut. Trooper Carter could have good news, but she doubted it.

She was right.

"Jennie, Luke," he greeted them, but his stern expression put them on alert. "I wanted to inform you that we found Randi Griggs's car an hour ago."

"Did you find who was driving it?" Jennie wrapped her arms around her waist like a shield.

"We didn't find the driver. We found Morgan in the car. He'd been shot point-blank."

Lights danced briefly before her eyes. Luke pushed her gently into a chair, then positioned himself behind her.

She drew in a deep breath. "Morgan was murdered? Why? What would be the point?"

"My guess? Whoever was giving the orders was upset that he failed to deliver you according to the plan."

That took a second or two to sink in. The horror that bled through her spirit at Steve's willingness to kill his own partners solidified her decision.

"We can't wait anymore." Standing, she faced Luke, tense and waiting. "We have to leave now. This minute. Steve knows we're in this area. We can't put your aunt and uncle in danger by staying."

Trooper Carter broke in. "I know you're anxious, Jennie. But the snow is falling down hard out there. And it's only going to get worse through the night. Leave early in the morning as planned. If you leave now, you might end up stuck on the side of the road and become an easy target."

ELEVEN

Jennie was ready to leave the moment the breakfast dishes were cleared. Trooper Carter arrived to tell them that there had been no additional sightings during the night. The weary look around his eyes told her he'd been on duty most of that time.

The longer they lingered, the greater the chance someone would sneak up on them again. And this time, maybe one of Luke's cousins or his uncle and aunt might get hurt. She refused to be the reason for his family to suffer, especially in light of how gracious and giving they'd been.

She also needed to put some space between LJ and this place. She had no idea who else was helping Steve. She could easily picture Pete Walsh being on his payroll. It was the kind of thing the man would do. The memory of his bitter smirk when he saw Luke all but clinched him as a viable suspect in her book.

No one was going to harm her family again. Not if she could stop it.

Luke put a single bag in the trunk of the car. When she tilted her head at him, he shrugged. "My jacket is ruined. *Onkel* Jed is lending me one of his. I have more clothes at *Mamm* and *Daed*'s *haus*. We'll also find you more clothes."

Jennie glanced down at the pink dress she was wearing. It was in good condition, although she would be happy to wash it. "Your cousin said I could borrow several of her dresses. She outgrew them."

Mary Alice Beiler was a good six inches taller than Jennie.

Luke made a face. "*Jah*, I know. But her dresses are all pink."

She waited, not understanding the point. She liked pink.

"New Wilmington is more—ah—traditional than Spartansburg and the surrounding areas."

"So?"

He shrugged. "Our rules are different. The woman usually wear dresses in any shade of blue or purple."

"Oh." There were rules about what colors she could wear? That had never crossed her mind. "Well, I guess I'll be changing clothes when we get to your parents' house."

There was no mistaking the look of relief that crossed his face. Did he fear she would protest or cause a fuss? She would do whatever she had to, wear whatever was necessary, if it would keep her son safe. "Color doesn't matter. All I care about is getting LJ out of this alive. Nothing else is important at the moment. I can wear any color I choose when this is all over."

A shadow passed over his face, but he didn't say anything more.

Trooper Carter was on his phone when they were ready to get underway, holding an intense conversation. She didn't want to interrupt but was itching to move before anything else happened. It took all her will to stand still and wait.

The moment he disconnected, he started toward her. As soon as he gave the all clear, she would gather LJ from Eleanor and they'd be off. Hopefully within the next five minutes.

"Jennie," Carter addressed her. "That was the Erie City Police Department. Oliver Deets has been picked up and is being held in the Erie County Jail."

Luke stepped up to her side. She grabbed on to his hand and held tight. Her sense of relief was short-lived. "Wait a minute. When was he picked up?"

"Early this morning. His alibi checks out. He was nowhere near here when Morgan attempted to kidnap your son."

"Which means…"

"Which means someone else was driving the car." Luke finished the words she was unwilling to say.

One more suspect crossed off the list.

Pete Walsh was looking more promising to her.

Trooper Carter wasn't convinced. "I'll keep looking into the guy, but as of now, he appears to be clean. Creepy, maybe, but nothing that would allow us to arrest him, or even issue a search warrant."

She needed to move before she crawled right out of her own skin. "Can we go now?"

When Carter agreed, she took off to gather her son. Eleanor handed him over with a smile, then she handed Jennie a basket. Jennie didn't need to lift the lid to tell it was filled with goodies. The aroma wafting from the basket was enough. The caring gesture touched her. She was so used to taking care of herself, it surprised her when someone tried to take care of her.

"Thanks for everything, Eleanor. I'm sorry we disrupted your house so much."

"Ach." Eleanor waved her apology aside. "Luke is family. We were happy to help. I will continue to pray for your strength and safety."

When Jennie started to turn to leave, Eleanor called out to her, "Remember, Jennie. *Gott* can do anything. He can make an impossible thing possible."

What did that mean? Jennie was still pondering Eleanor's words as she buckled LJ into his booster seat. Unlike the day before, he was not smiling.

"I don't wanna go for a ride." That bottom lip stuck out as far as he could stick it. "I wanna go home."

So did she. She held in her smile. "Don't you want to go on another mission, LJ? Meet your grandparents?"

That made him pause. "I have a grandma? Like Noah?"

"Noah's a friend from preschool," she informed Luke, who was settling into the passenger seat. "Noah stays with his grandmother while his mom works."

"Jah, you have grandparents, LJ. But in an Amish *haus*, your grandmother is called *Grossmammi*, and grandfather is *Grossdawdi*. Can you remember that?"

LJ's little face scrunched up. "I don't know. It sounds strange."

Luke chuckled. "Maybe so. But you'll get used to it."

The little boy thought about it for a moment, then shrugged. Jennie could see that he had dismissed the subject already. When his stomach started rumbling, she knew why. Before LJ could start complaining, she told Luke about the basket his aunt had sent with her.

"Why don't you open up the basket and see what she sent?" She glanced back in the rearview mirror at her son. "Daddy is looking for something for you to eat. Be patient just a moment more."

"Aha!"

Luke's shout had her jumping in her seat.

"What?"

He looked sheepish. "Sorry. She packed some of her cinnamon rolls for us. Those are my favorites, and she knows it."

Shaking her head, Jennie laughed. "You scared me. You know that? But as long as we are talking cinnamon rolls, I'll forgive you. Hand one over."

Grinning, he passed the treats around.

"There are wet wipes in the glove compartment."

Content and no longer hungry, LJ drifted off to sleep in the back seat. Jennie sighed, grateful for small favors. They drove through Meadville.

"Look at all the decorations," she mused. "Christmas is only a few days away. I can't believe it."

"I hope that the danger is passed by then."

She couldn't have agreed more. Except, she didn't want to think about what that meant for them after the danger was past. But she knew.

It would all be over.

Jennie had gone quiet. Her face had lost the animation displayed while they were eating. What was going through her mind? Luke knew that look.

When she bit her lip, he gasped, his mind flooded with an overload of memories. So many, so fast. Jennie was in many of them. He saw her in her wedding dress. Her on the beach. Laughing. Crying. The memories were flashing in his mind so fast he grew dizzy.

Squeezing his eyes closed, he pressed his hands to his face, trying to slow the onslaught. It was futile.

He was barely aware of the movement of the car as it came to a stop.

A warm hand on his arm jerked him out of his reverie. He raised his face to see Jennie, barely aware of the tears on his own face.

"I remember. I remember everything."

The ache at what he had lost tortured him. His bride. He remembered how much he loved her then. And he knew that he was falling in love with her again. Now that it was too late. Letting her go would destroy him, but he couldn't see that he had a choice. He couldn't go back to live in her world. It wasn't who he was anymore. But at the same time, he couldn't ask her to move to his permanently.

When he could finally breathe again, he leaned his head back against the headrest. "I'm okay. Go. We can't sit here."

She waited a moment, her eyes scanning his face with laser precision, as if to catalog each line and tear. Finally, she nodded and flipped on the blinker before smoothly merging back in with the traffic.

Sighing, he moved his head to look around. His eyes were raw, his emotions drained. In five minutes, he'd come to face everything he'd lost.

Out the window, he saw the signs for I-79. He sat up straighter, pushing his own small problems to the side. "Get on 79, head south like you're going to Pittsburgh."

Without comment, she did as he asked. Once on I-79, his eyes widened.

"I don't recall the traffic being this heavy when I headed north to find you."

"It's two days before Christmas. People are traveling. Just be glad we're making the trip today and not tomorrow. Tomorrow we'd be packed in like sardines in a tin."

He shuddered. "I hate feeling closed in."

"Yeah. Me, too." She changed lanes to pass a slow-moving car. "So, if you have your memories back, do you remember what happened to you?"

He paused, pulling the threads of that day together in his mind. "I think so. I was at work, and my shift ended. I'd forgotten to put gas in my car that morning."

She laughed softly. "You did that more than once. Always waiting to the last moment."

"Well, this time, I waited too long. When I went to start my car, it turned over and died. No gas. I wasn't worried. The factory I worked at was only a mile from a gas station and it was a nice day. I left my car and grabbed the gas can, figuring I'd go get a gallon, enough to get going. I was halfway there when I heard the explosion."

She sucked in her breath. "Did you know what it was?"

"*Jah*, I knew. My plant was a chemical plant. What else would have exploded? I turned to run back. I must have been hit by a car. Whoever hit me obviously didn't stick around to see if I was alive. When I woke up, I had no idea where I was. Or how old I was. I thought I was only seventeen. I hitched a ride to my parents' *haus*."

And lost so much.

"I always wondered what had happened to you," she mused. "Your phone was in your car, which suffered some damage from falling debris. The police never found any other evidence of you. It didn't make sense to me, but my whole life came apart that day. All I had was the knowledge that I was pregnant. I hadn't even told you yet."

They both fell silent.

"Umm, Luke?"

"Jah?"

"I think we're being followed."

He pushed himself up to look over the headrest. As she weaved in and out of the traffic, picking up speed, the pickup truck behind them kept pace.

"Jah, we're being followed."

Her face settled into grim lines. She pushed her foot down on the gas, and he heard the rev of the motor as her car sped up. Glancing back, he saw that the pickup was coming closer.

"We have to get off the interstate," he decided. "We're trapped here. If the traffic backs up at all, we'd be easy targets if he decided to get out of his truck and come for us."

"That's what I'm afraid of." Her voice was calm, but her knuckles on the steering wheel were white.

"Get off at the first exit that doesn't lead to another interstate or highway. We need a road that has intersections."

She nodded. "Or at least the possibility that it will lead to a police station. I doubt anyone would be so bold as to follow us in there."

Luke prayed in his mind as Jennie continued to weave in and out of traffic. Five minutes flowed into ten, and still the truck followed them. Jennie moved back into the right lane. As the pickup moved toward them, a large bus merged onto the road from the on-ramp.

For a moment, the pickup was out of sight.

"Now!" Luke shouted. "Go there!"

There was an exit. Jennie jerked the wheel and zoomed onto the ramp. Luke looked back. The truck was starting to pass the exit. Hopefully, he'd drive on by and they'd be free of him.

Horns blared as the truck slammed on its brakes and backed up, then turned onto the exit.

If there had been any doubt as to whether or not the pickup was really following them, it was gone. Jennie barely slowed at the light near the base of the ramp. She flew down the road. This was a smaller street with less traffic. The benefit was there weren't as many cars to navigate around. The downfall was there weren't as many to act as a barrier, either.

Without warning, Jennie skidded onto a side road, dirt and snow flying up, the wheels spinning in the mush for an instant. Luke looked back and saw the truck wasn't behind them. It was too early to say they were out of danger.

She spun around the next curve.

There was a dog standing in the middle of the road.

With a horrified yell, she jerked the wheel.

Luke felt the car skid beneath them. "Hold on!"

He braced his arm against the dash, reaching back to touch LJ, to catch him if he needed to.

Jennie's car slid across the road and landed in a ditch. The hood was buried up to the windshield in snow.

They needed to move. If they were still here when the pickup truck arrived, they would be sitting targets.

TWELVE

LJ was sobbing. Luke forced his door open. When he stepped out of the car, he sank down to his knees in snow. Bracing his hands against the side of the car, he worked his way toward the back of the car, battling the drifts and the thorny branches lining the road. By the time he got to the trunk, his feet were like blocks of ice stuffed into his boots and he had scratches on every inch of visible skin.

Jennie met him with LJ in her arms. She seemed to have weathered the short walk better than he had. Her side of the car had far fewer bushes on it. He was glad of that.

"Leave everything you don't need in the car," he said.

She patted the straps of the backpack she was carrying. It doubled as LJ's bag. "I put my money and my phone in here. I'm ready."

He took LJ from her and together they ran across the road. There was an old tractor path along the side of the road. It veered off a couple hundred yards away, but was still far too visible for his peace of mind. When she started walking toward it, he reached out and grabbed her hand to stop her.

"I don't want him to be able to follow us with a truck." He tugged her toward the trees.

He helped her climb up the steep incline. She slipped once, and her pink dress became splotched with muddy stains where her knees hit the ground. She didn't let it stop her. By sheer dint of will, the three of them were soon into the trees, well hidden from the road.

"We should do our best to step where there isn't any snow or soft mud," Jennie said. "That way we won't leave tracks for him to follow."

"*Gut* idea."

It was harder to walk in the more overgrown parts. Roots made tripping a constant hazard. Plus, it was difficult to remain quiet when they were constantly tripping.

A deep rumble came from the direction of the road they'd left. They stilled briefly. Jennie whispered to LJ that he had to stay as quiet as he could. When he started to pout, she leaned closer.

"There's a bad man after us, honey. We have to stay quiet so he doesn't hear us."

LJ's eyes grew wide, and his little face grew taut. He stayed silent, though.

When the motor didn't pass by but seemed to stop in place, their gazes locked. Luke nodded at Jennie, indicating with his chin that they needed to keep moving. The truck had stopped at their car.

They walked until they came to the next road. Luke didn't want to stay out in the open. He had no idea where they were. They kept moving.

A few minutes later, they heard someone crashing through the woods behind them. Whoever had been following them hadn't given up, but had entered the woods.

Luke led them across the road and into a small forest, fragrant with all manner of evergreen trees: pine, spruce, any kind of fir one could imagine. The trees were spaced at equal intervals. Every once in a while, he'd see a stump where a tree had been cut down.

"Mama," LJ whispered. "We're in a Christmas tree farm."

So they were.

"Jennie." Luke waited until she looked at him. "If you turned your phone on, do you think we could call for help?"

Her eyes brightened. She rooted around in the bag for her phone and turned it on. It seemed to take forever to power up. Her expression dimmed. "No bars. Figures."

Disappointed, he nodded. Maybe they could find someone who worked here. He doubted there was a phone on the premises. It looked like a business where people came and got their own trees.

"Let's keep moving." Luke placed a hand firmly on Jennie's back, urging her to continue walking. They passed a few last-minute shoppers, out looking for that perfect tree. Each time they pasted smiles on their faces and kept going, aware what a mess they must have looked with their mud-encrusted clothes and twigs stuck in their hair.

Luke squinted at Jennie.

"What?" she hissed at him.

"I don't mean to be rude, but did you know you have sap in your hair?"

LJ snickered.

"Ha-ha. You two are so funny. And yes, I know. There were some ferocious trees in the woods earlier."

He laughed.

A bullet smashed into the tree next to him.

The couple two trees away screamed and ran. Luke grabbed up LJ. Jennie started running, and he was right behind her, zigzagging their way through the trees.

Jennie veered to the left. He followed. The trees became denser. It would be more difficult for anyone to shoot them here. Another bullet crashed into a tree. Well, more difficult to shoot with any accuracy.

They bolted, ducking around the trees. After a few minutes, the number of trees began to thin. Up ahead was a brightly decorated tree, full of ornate bulbs and cheery lights. Beside it stood a large sign that read O'Malley's Trees. Glancing around, Luke tried to see if he could spot the owner or a worker. Then he looked closer at the sign and nearly groaned. *We follow the honor system.* Customers were free to pick out their trees and were asked to drop the money to pay for them in the slot of a large container. Luke tugged on Jennie's hand. They squatted down behind the tree and waited. Sweat was sticking to his collar. When LJ put his head on Luke's shoulder and plopped his thumb in his mouth, Luke bent his head and prayed for the danger to go past them.

Jennie was squeezed in tight next to him. He could feel her warmth through his jacket. He could also feel that she was trembling. Whether with cold, fear or both, he couldn't tell. Her face, however, gave nothing away. Probably being strong for LJ. She wouldn't want her son to see her scared.

A family of five entered the gate. When the twin daughters saw the tree, they begged their parents to let them see it up close. The mother, father and all three children stood by the tree, oohing and aahing over the ornaments. They effectively blocked anyone from seeing the sign. Or the three people hiding behind it.

A man crashed through the farm and came right up to the decorated tree, his cruel gaze scanning the surrounding area.

Jennie gasped softly but quickly buried the sound by turning her face into Luke's shoulder. She had recognized the man, whoever he was. Luke couldn't risk asking her who it was now.

LJ lifted his head.

Oh, not now. Please not now.

"Ma—"

Jennie swept him close, murmuring in his ear. Her hair tickled Luke's nose. He scolded himself for being tempted to sniff just to see if her hair still smelled like vanilla.

"Not now, baby," she breathed in LJ's ear. "The bad man's right over there. Please don't move. Play statue."

Luke had never heard of the game "statue," but LJ clearly understood it. He went absolutely still, barely even breathing. Luke was so proud of him, and impressed, too. It was no easy task to stay still when something exciting or scary was happening.

After what seemed a very long time, but was only actually a minute or two, the man turned and stormed out the exit. They remained hidden for another couple of minutes to make sure he was really gone. When Luke was confident that he'd actually left, he led his family through the exit.

They were out in the open now. The sky was heavy with clouds. It looked like more snow was on the way. Instead of dirt road, the one in front of him was paved. That meant they were closer to town on this side of the woods. The downside was paved roads would be easier for their pursuers to drive on.

"How do they keep finding us?" Jennie wondered.

Luke's brow furrowed. "I don't know much about such things, but is it possible that they are tracking your phone?"

She shook her head. "It was off until we were in the woods. Remember? Trooper Carter wanted me to be untraceable."

"Except someone was tracing you."

"Hold on." Jennie spent a few minutes going through the items in her bag. "I don't see anything suspicious in here"

Frustrated, he shook his head. They'd have to think about it, but right now, they needed to get out of here. He had a feeling the man with the gun hadn't given up. He'd probably gone back to get his truck. Which didn't leave them that much time.

Luke's head lifted when he heard a trickling sound. *Water!*

He pointed toward the noise. Jennie's eyes followed the direction of his finger and she nodded. Together, they headed that way. The steady gurgle of water nearby grew louder with each step they took. After a few minutes, they stood looking down at a creek, merrily babbling over the rocks and boulders in its bed. He could see a road crossing over the stream. Even as they watched, a car drove over it. A few seconds later, another car went by, heading in the opposite direction.

"I wonder if we should try to go over that bridge," Jennie mused.

It wasn't exactly what he'd call a bridge. It was level with the rest of the road. He shrugged, and they headed toward it. At the base of the bridge, they paused, trying to decide in which direction they should go.

The air was split by the roar of a truck coming down the road. In a minute, he'd be to the bridge. There was no way to know if it was the man who'd followed them into the Christmas tree farm, but they couldn't take the chance.

Scrambling down the bank, Luke gestured for them to go into the shallow stream. Under the road, a culvert provided structure and allowed the water to flow from one side of the bridge to the other.

"There. We'll go through the culvert."

Jennie crouched in the entrance of the culvert so she was hidden from any vehicles passing overhead. She didn't want to enter the culvert. Just the thought had her breaking out in a cold sweat. The large hollow stone structure reminded Jennie of a tomb. It was cold, damp and the sound of the water running under the bridge was amplified.

She wouldn't be able to stand up straight inside it. And the noise! It was so loud in here. Jennie had never liked tunnels or caves. She hated small spaces. Another car crossed overhead. She squeezed her eyes shut. The culvert sounded like it would collapse at any moment. Jennie could feel it vibrating around her.

Don't go there. They should be fine if they stayed where they were. If it started to collapse, they could get out in time. Maybe. Besides, it was made of cement. What could be stronger?

She was repeating her mantra when Luke moved in closer. Normally, she enjoyed his closeness; now he was invading her personal breathing space.

"Who was he, Jennie? The man in the truck. I know you recognized him."

She twisted her lips into a smile, though it was probably not a pretty one. "I only sort of knew him. I'm not even sure of his name. This guy moved into the empty apartment on the first floor of my building a while back. We never said more than hi. I had heard that he worked nights and slept most of the day. I never suspected him of anything. The day that Steve escaped, I almost ran him down on my stairs on my way out to get to LJ's school. Now I wonder what he was doing there. Has he been keeping tabs on me this past year, too?"

Luke thought about that a moment. "I don't think he's going to give up searching. Not anytime soon."

She hated it, but she had to agree. "You're probably right. And he's probably told someone else that we've been spotted in the area. I think we should accept that we can't go back for my car."

That had never really been an option, but she liked her car. It had been with her a long time and it was perfect for her life.

"Jennie, I think your car was how they found us." That got her attention fast.

"I'm not following. What do you mean?"

Luke pointed in the direction they'd come from. "Think about it. They've found us no matter where we went. What if there's some kind of tracking device in your car? If that guy was at your apartment, keeping tabs on you, isn't it possible he did something to your car so that when Steve gave the order, they'd be able to find you?"

Her heart sank. It made sense. "So, what? Do we

walk to your parents' house? We have a four-year-old, Luke. It's too cold. And we're wet."

"*Nee*, we won't walk all the way to my parents' *haus*. Just far enough for you to use your phone. We can call Trooper Carter. Then we can get a ride the rest of the way."

"Okay. Well, should we go up—"

He was shaking his head. "Let's go through the culvert here. Then we can follow the stream for a bit. We'll call Trooper Carter as soon as you have signal."

"Through the culvert? Luke, it's not safe to travel through a culvert." She was starting to feel panic bubbling up inside. It was popping in her stomach and traveling along her nerves. Sure, it wasn't that long. Only the length of a two-lane street. But it could collapse at any moment and they'd might never make it out.

"*Nee*, it's perfectly safe. What could happen to it? These walls are pure concrete." He kicked at the wall.

She wanted to keep protesting. Wanted to tell him that she couldn't bear to be closed in. She opened her mouth to do just that.

What if someone is waiting up there? What if LJ or Luke get injured because you were a coward?

She swallowed her protests. Now was the time to put her trust in God to the test. He could get her through this. Taking a deep breath, she followed Luke and LJ into the dark culvert. It was difficult to walk crouched down as she was. She felt like she was going to lose her balance and tumble forward. The overhead rumble of a vehicle stopped her cold. Inside the culvert, it sounded like an earthquake. Jennie grabbed hold of LJ to protect him with her body.

The noise stopped. She could breathe again. They

were halfway through. She could see the light at the other end. Her breathing was loud in too small space. It was ridiculous to feel like there was no oxygen when she could clearly see the opening ahead of them.

"Can we go any faster?" There was a note of panic in her voice. She winced. She hadn't meant to react so poorly.

"Jennie, are you claustrophobic?" Luke leaned in to see her more clearly. "I don't remember you being bothered by small spaces before."

She narrowed her eyes to focus her glare. "You never wondered why I was so adamant about not taking the elevator in the apartment?"

His mouth fell open as understanding dawned. "I thought you wanted the exercise. That's what you said."

"Yeah, well, I did, but I wanted to avoid that narrow box held up on unreliable cables even more."

"We're almost there. Hold on a few more seconds."

She blew out a hard breath. "Just move. We're right behind you."

The water whooshed around her ankles. Within minutes, they were nearly numb. Pebbles and small rocks were carried in with the water and deposited. They made the floor uneven and difficult to walk on.

"See that light, LJ? We're almost there."

She wasn't sure if she was reassuring herself or her son. Probably a little of both.

When they reached the end, her limbs trembled from fatigue and relief. Luke climbed out and reached back to pull LJ out. He hugged the boy to him briefly, before turning back to help Jennie down. When her feet touched the ground on the bank of the creek, her knees started to give out. Luke caught her to him and held her against him.

His heartbeat in her ear, strong and steady, warmed her more than a down-filled parka would. She rested there for a few seconds before pulling away. He let her go, but she thought she could sense some reluctance.

Was it her imagination, or was he as drawn to her as she was to him?

Was there any way they could both get through this without their hearts being broken?

THIRTEEN

Jennie couldn't remember the last time she'd been so cold. The water from the creek had soaked into the hem of her dress and sopped down into her boots. Her black cloak, the same kind she'd seen the Amish women near her home wear when they were out and about in winter, was so wet that it weighed her down like she was carrying a sack full of rocks.

For all of her discomfort, though, she was too happy to be free and in a wide open space to complain. If they stayed along the creek, they'd move away from the road. There weren't as many trees, but it would be hard for someone to follow them in a vehicle. She sighed, grateful to be on the other side of the culvert.

LJ didn't feel the same. He began to whine and whimper. Her heart broke for her little boy. He was cold, hungry and tired. She had no idea where they were. Pulling out her phone, she wanted to dance when she saw three bars. Quickly tapping her apps icon, she searched for their location with the maps application.

What she saw didn't make her feel any better.

"Luke, we're still half an hour from New Wilmington if we were in a car. There's no way we can walk that distance, not as we are. LJ will get sick."

Luke frowned at them, his concern evident. "Can we start walking? Now that you have service, you can call the police as we walk, and they can send someone for us."

She didn't see any other choice.

The wind had picked up, blowing icy air on them as they walked. The bitter chill was causing her to tremble and shake. She took LJ's hand in hers. It was a block of ice. Tucking her phone under her arm, she took his hand in both of hers and rubbed them together to warm it. Luke copied her action on the boy's other side. After a few moments she took her right hand away and pulled out her phone again.

Jennie tried to speed-dial Trooper Carter one-handed. It took her three tries before she was able to correctly enter her pass code to unlock the phone. Tears came to her eyes when he finally picked up his phone and answered.

"Jennie? What's wrong? Are you in New Wilmington yet?" he demanded.

It took her a moment to control her voice enough to answer him. She was suddenly so weary. "Not yet. We ran into some trouble."

Luke snorted beside her. When she shot him a glance, he rolled his eyes at her.

Okay, so that was an understatement.

Trooper Carter's voice sharpened. "Trouble? Explain."

Jennie started from the beginning, telling him about the man who had chased them, the car crashing into the ditch and their flight on foot. When she finished with their present predicament, he barked out a few questions about their exact location.

"I'm putting you on speaker," he said. "Hold on." She could hear him set the phone down on his desk and then his fingers were tapping on his keyboard. "Okay, Jennie. I have you. Listen, I'm sending a car to pick you up. Keep walking south. A car should be there in about five to ten minutes. They'll have emergency blankets to help you warm up. I'm also sending a tow truck to see if we can get your car back here. We'll check it for any type of tracking device."

"Thank you." She'd welcome a ride in a police car right now. Anything to get LJ out of the cold.

"Stay on the line with me. This man, the one from your apartment. I need a physical description. What did he look like?"

She gathered her thoughts. "He wasn't that tall. Five-six, maybe. A couple of inches taller than me. Blondish brown hair. Maybe about to his ears. He sort of had a beard. Not a full one. But a little more than just scruff, you know?"

"What about body build?"

"Average. Not someone you'd pay much attention to on the street."

Trooper Carter shot off a few more questions. Which apartment did he live in; when had he moved in; anything odd she'd noticed about him? Jennie answered his questions as much as possible, but wasn't sure she'd given him anything that helpful.

"Good job, Jennie. You keep walking. When you get to Luke's parents' house, I want you to send me a text. I have the address. Keep this phone on you. I will be sending a text or calling."

"Umm, that might be a problem." She saw Luke turning his head to look at her. "Luke's family is Amish, as you know. I'm not sure how I'll be able to charge my phone. I charged it as much as I could before we had to leave my car, but it's only about half charged now."

Luke shook his head at her. "There will be no electricity at their *haus*. Not even in my *daed*'s workshop."

With a sinking feeling, she relayed that information to Trooper Carter.

He was silent a moment while he processed this information. "Okay. I want you to turn off your phone as soon as you arrive safely. The troopers who pick you up can let me know you've arrived. Turn your phone on twice a day to check for texts or send me one telling me you're okay. This might buy us a few days. Once your phone is completely dead, we'll have to think of something else."

She relayed the information to Luke.

"There's a phone in our barn for business purposes. We also have a community phone booth near the *haus*. We'll be able to call if we need to."

"I heard that," Trooper Carter said. "The police should be nearly to you."

Jennie could see them now. "Hey, Carter. I see a cruiser coming toward us. It's pulling over to the side."

"Good. I'm going to hang up now. Let them take care of you. You stay safe and be vigilant. Constantly on your guard. I mean it, Jennie. We still don't know how many people are involved in this mess."

She didn't need to be reminded to be careful. She wasn't sure she'd be able to fully trust anyone ever again after the chaos of the past few days. People she'd thought were just ordinary folks had turned into cold-blooded killers. Her faith in her ability to judge character was sadly diminished.

The trooper in the car identified herself as Trooper Lisa Jones. Jennie liked her immediately. She was efficient and calm as she helped them remove their wet coats and handed out blankets. She had also grabbed some sandwiches from the deli at a nearby gas station and some bottled water.

"I wasn't sure what you'd like, and they didn't have much of a variety. I hope this works."

"Mmm." Jennie nodded as she bit into her tuna fish sandwich. "This is perfect, thank you."

She was more thankful than ever that LJ was not a picky eater. He'd eat almost anything when he was hungry. Within minutes, they were on their way. Trooper Jones turned the heat up to full blast. "There's heated seats, too. So get as comfortable as you can."

No longer hungry or cold, LJ's natural curiosity rose to the surface. He peppered the trooper with a constant barrage of questions as she headed toward their final destination.

Jennie met Luke's gaze over his head. His blue eyes warmed her as they caressed her face. "Okay now?"

She nodded in response to his soft murmur.

"It will be fine now," he promised. "My parents will help us. It will please *Mamm* to be able to spoil LJ for a few days."

A few days. Would that be all? Or would they be in hiding much longer than that? It was hard not knowing when, or indeed if, her world would ever right itself again. Could she go back to her old job, her old life as if nothing had changed?

Jennie kept her questions and her doubts sealed up

behind her closed lips as she smiled at the man sitting so near. She no longer had any answers. This man had stormed into her life to rescue her. He had, but he'd also stolen her heart in the process.

She didn't know how she'd go back to her life when this was over. How was she supposed to pretend to be happy when the man she loved was living his life, hours away?

They were safe. For the moment.

Luke stared at the woman sitting just a foot away from him. Her face had turned to watch the passing scenery. The serenity in her expression drew him in. It was hard to believe only an hour ago they'd been crawling through that culvert.

Ditching her car was the right decision. He knew it was. The man who'd chased them through the Christmas tree farm was probably still looking for them, even as they were safe and secure inside a police vehicle speeding to his parents' home. To do it over again, maybe they should have asked Trooper Carter to find them an escort to New Wilmington. They couldn't have expected what had happened.

Jennie was filthy. Her hair was stringy from the cold and wet weather, her cheeks were streaked with dirt, and she still had some sap on the side of her face. Not to mention the scratches and scrapes she'd obtained during their flight.

He'd never seen anyone more beautiful. Her strength staggered him. Her willingness to follow him into the culvert, sacrificing her own comfort and putting herself through what must have been an agony in light of her phobia, humbled him. He never could have expected that much trust from her.

His gaze dropped to the top of LJ's head. LJ had been fantastic through this. While Luke knew it had started as an adventure for the four-year-old, they'd asked him to cope with a lot. Not that there had been a choice. But he'd come through with so little fussing.

Luke had an amazing family.

For now.

His heart ached with love for these two people. Two people that had been strangers only days before. Now they were the most important people in his world. What would he do when they returned home?

He didn't like the idea of them going back to that apartment. Not after all that had happened.

It wouldn't be his call to make. The thought was devastating. He tore his mind away from it. He had to get them through the next few days, or however long it took until the police could do their job and catch those who were after his Jennie.

In his mind, he could see Steve Curtis. The man was handsome, charismatic even. But Luke had seen him for the monster he truly was. If Luke hadn't been there that day ten years ago, Steve would have killed Jennie. He knew it.

How did such a man continue to move around and gather supporters?

But clearly, he had.

Suddenly, Luke became aware of his surroundings.

"We're close," he told Jennie and LJ. "See that buggy?" He pointed out the window to a buggy that was black on the bottom and a medium tan color, almost a burnt orange, on top.

"Why does it look so much different than the one your uncle has?" Jennie combed her hair back behind her ears. The *kapp* she'd been wearing was no longer the crisp white starched *kapp* she'd started out with that morning.

"That's what our buggies look like in our communities here. I don't know why. I do know that they are different from every other Amish community in North America."

He tried to imagine how she saw his people. The men in their dark trousers and suspenders, and the women with their blue and purple dresses and dark cloaks. To him, these were good, hardworking people who tried to live as the *gut* Lord wished. They valued family, hard work and simple things.

But to her, how did they did they seem?

It shouldn't be important how she viewed his family and community.

But it was.

When they pulled into the drive at his parents' farm, Luke sat up. Had Raymond managed to explain to *Mamm* and *Daed* what had happened? How much had his brother said?

Probably very little, he realized. This was his situation. Raymond wouldn't have wanted to tell them too much. Just enough to let them know that Luke felt he was doing the correct thing.

When he stepped from the car, he knew he'd been right.

His *mamm* and *daed* came out onto the wide wraparound porch, their eyes curious and cautious. At first, they glanced over Jennie and LJ without any recognition that the boy they were seeing was their grandson.

Luke and Jennie thanked Trooper Jones for her help. As she backed out of the driveway, they headed toward the small group waiting for them on the porch.

But then Luke's mother gasped. Her gaze flew back to LJ and devoured him, as if she were trying to make sense of what her eyes were seeing.

"Luke." Her calm voice demanded he tell her the truth. "Luke, the *kind*. He looks like you did when you were small."

He should have known her sharp mind and perceptive eyes would have caught the resemblance.

"*Jah*. LJ, *cumme*." He motioned the four-year-old to his side. LJ ran to his father. "LJ, I want to introduce your *grossmammi* and your *grossdawdi*. These are your grandparents."

FOURTEEN

His poor *mamm* gasped, hands flying to her mouth in shock. His father's face grew somber. Luke had much explaining to do. Raymond, he noticed, had come out and then discreetly disappeared.

Coward.

Jennie moved to stand behind her son, hands on his shoulders. Luke's *mamm* took in her bedraggled appearance, and her keen sense of hospitality took over.

"Luke, bring them inside. They look ready to keel over. We can talk in the kitchen."

"It's going to be all right." He gestured them to follow. Jennie's glance was wry and a bit on the wary side. He couldn't blame her. He wasn't sure how his parents would react when they discovered she was *Englisch* and not Plain.

Well, they'd soon know, one way or another.

In the kitchen, his *mamm* fussed over LJ, washing off his face and smoothing back his hair. She brought out some cookies she'd made earlier in the week. Luke's *mamm* loved baking, and at Christmastime, she made lots of cookies.

"Your sister Anna's teacher was here today. The *Englisch* one. I gave her some cookies."

Luke's youngest sister, Anna, had Down syndrome. She had a special speech teacher who came to the *haus* to work with her twice a month.

"Miss Kelley? Why was she here today? Aren't they on Christmas break?"

"*Jah*. She was dropping off papers. Anna won't be getting speech anymore."

That was *gut* news. Anna had made great progress in the past two years. Her speech would always be challenging for outsiders to understand, but here within the family, she was loved and understood. His sister would never want for care. Plain families always took care of their own.

After a few minutes, his *mamm* was clearly getting around to asking the questions he'd almost been dreading. Before she could begin, he smoothly nudged his way into introductions first. "*Mamm, Daed*, this is Jennie."

"Jennie," Luke's father greeted her. "I'm Jonas Beiler, and this is my wife, Sarah. How is it that your son is my grandson?"

Well. That was to the point.

"*Daed*, do you recall those years that I was gone?" Dumb question. *Ach*, of course they remembered.

"*Jah*," his *mamm* said. Only one word. That might be bad.

"Well, I had left the Amish world. Jennie, she and I met when I worked with *Onkel* Jed. She's *Englisch*."

"*Englisch!* Why is she dressed like so?" His *mamm* seemed more bothered by that fact than any other.

"I'm getting to it. Let me explain. See, when I left, I met Jennie. And we, um, we got married."

The silence that fell had the weight of an explosion. He could feel the pressure of it pushing down on him.

"Married. To an *Englischer.*"

"*Jah, Daed.* Married. When I was injured, she was told I was dead. I never knew about LJ."

"Son," Jonas began, staring at Jennie with suspicion. "Are you sure you were married?"

Jennie's face flushed deep red.

Mortified, Luke burst out, "*Daed!* Of course. I believe her. And this day, my memories have returned. All of them."

"Luke." Jennie got his attention in the pause that followed that announcement. "Maybe we should tell them the reason we're here. Before we tell them anything else."

He nodded. She was right. Once they knew that their grandson was in danger, his parents were sure to be more willing to hear what he had to say. Quickly, he started with the day he'd seen Steve's image on the television and brought them up-to-date on all that had happened since then.

They were both horrified to hear of the multiple attacks on Jennie and the attempts to kidnap LJ. When his mother heard LJ stood for Luke Junior, she had to wipe away her tears on her apron.

"I'm not surprised that my brother would help in this way," Jonas commented when Luke mentioned staying at Jed's *haus.* "He is a *gut* man, and willing to help anyone in need."

Luke noticed his *daed* didn't say if he approved of his brother's involvement. Jennie, he could see, had schooled her features into a polite mask. He knew she was guarding her feelings. His parents' shock must have wounded her.

When he told them about going through the culvert, and Jennie's bravery, his mother broke through the awkwardness to reach out and pat her shoulder. "You poor child. You've been through so much. *Cumme.* We'll get you cleaned up and dressed in fresh clothes. My daughter Theresa's dresses might fit you." She gave Luke a calm stare. "You should go clean up. Then you can help your brothers with the chores before dinner."

Just like that, it was decided. Jennie and LJ were staying with them. His *mamm* put Jennie and LJ in with Theresa. It would be crowded, but they would be warm and dry.

It felt good to be clean again. Luke hurried to the barn to assist Raymond and their oldest brother, Simon. His brothers weren't shy about asking questions. Fortunately, there was too much work for them to spend too much time quizzing him. Their father would not appreciate it if they fell behind on the chores.

When he came inside for dinner, he placed his hat on the hook inside the door, just as his *daed* and his brothers did. He was greeted first by Anna. His sweet sister was only ten, but she had the innocence of a much younger child. She had the most loving heart he'd ever known.

"Luke!" She was almost jiggling up and down in her excitement at seeing him. "You're home!"

"*Jah*, I'm home. Were you *gut* while I was gone?"

She ducked her head. His parents encouraged her to use her voice to communicate, but she frequently responded with nonverbal gestures. It was fine. They understood her and loved her the way she was.

When he entered the kitchen and saw LJ and Jennie, his pulse took off. He'd enjoyed seeing Jennie dressed Amish before, but seeing her now in his home, wearing a dark purple dress and a fresh white *kapp*, he knew he'd never seen anyone prettier. He dropped his eyes so he would not stare at her. But he wanted to.

As the family sat around the table, they bowed their heads in silent prayer. When his father said "Amen," it was time to eat.

Jennie and LJ were both quiet that night. He guessed they were both feeling shy. They were also most likely exhausted from their long journey.

Luke was exhausted, but had trouble falling asleep. His mind wouldn't shut down enough for him to rest.

He kept seeing the face of the man who'd followed them into the Christmas tree farm. Where was he now? Had Trooper Carter been able to find him, or was he still at large, hunting them down?

Jennie awoke in the middle of the night, her heart pounding in her chest. It took her a few moments to get her bearings and figure out where she was. When she realized that she was in Luke's home, sleeping in his sister's room, she released the deep breath she'd been holding and relaxed back into the mattress.

It was still dark outside. LJ was snoring lightly beside her. She tucked the blanket around him and tried to settle down again. Luke had been right. His parents' house was not as bright as his uncle's had been. Still, she appreciated them allowing her and LJ to stay. Once the shock had worn off, his parents and siblings had all welcomed them, although she sensed their caution. She doubted if they knew what to do about the fact that their Amish son was legally married to a non-Amish woman.

She managed to fall asleep again, but woke up shortly after dawn. When she heard people moving about in the house, she got up and helped LJ get ready. When Theresa offered to take the child downstairs, Jennie accepted gratefully. When they were gone, she dressed quickly. After rebraiding her hair, she pinned the braid up and then donned the white *kapp* that Sarah had given her.

She actually liked the *kapp* in an odd sort of way. When Sarah had explained that in the Amish world, the women keep their hair hidden from all men except their husbands, she had liked the idea. It might have seemed old-fashioned, but she liked how it emphasized the unique bond and intimacy that existed in marriage.

The *kapp* was also different than any she'd ever seen. Not that she'd seen that many.

She walked down into the kitchen and was startled to see that both Theresa and Anna had their long, straight hair hanging down their backs.

"*Gut* morning, Jennie." Sarah finished combing Anna's hair, then she deftly braided it. When she placed the *kapp* on the girl's head, Jennie remembered her thought upstairs.

"Sarah, I was curious, why are your *kapps* different than the others I've seen?"

Sarah smiled and picked up the *kapp* that Theresa had set down. "See this?" She pointed to several small pleats around the edge. "We make our own *kapps*. Each one has sixty pleats."

"Sixty!" The amount of work and care that took seemed formidable.

Sarah handed the *kapp* to Theresa. Jennie watched the blonde girl put it on. Theresa was probably around sixteen or so, she guessed.

"Do you sew, Jennie?" Sarah began setting the table for breakfast. Jennie quickly offered to help.

"I can mend things. But I've never sewn an entire outfit."

"We sew all our clothes," Theresa said, joining the conversation as she poured hot coffee into a carafe to set on the table.

"*Jah*, we do. Theresa is seventeen now, so she joins in the singings. When she gets married, she'll sew her own wedding dress."

Theresa blushed.

"Singings?"

"*Jah*. Singings are social gatherings for our young people who are old enough to court and start searching for a spouse."

Jennie tried to wrap her mind around the idea. Seventeen seemed so young, although she'd only just turned nineteen when she'd married Luke.

The realization that she had fallen for him again made her uncomfortable, so she thrust it from her mind. There were more important things than romance to consider at the moment. Staying alive was at the top of the list.

When the men joined them for breakfast, she was pleased to note how happy LJ seemed.

"Mama!" He zoomed right up to her. "Guess what?"

"What?"

"There are puppies in the barn. I helped *Onkel* Raymond name them. One of them is Buster."

Of course. Did *Onkel* Raymond remind her son that the puppies would remain here when they left? She aimed a level stare at the man.

He grinned back. "They are blue heeler pups. Buster is a pretty little girl pup. She's not really a pup anymore. There's a younger litter. She's almost a year old."

She laughed. LJ didn't realize that Buster was the name for a boy dog. The innocence of it all stole her breath.

After breakfast, she ran up to her room and grabbed her phone. Then she and Luke grabbed their coats and boots and managed to steal away to the barn for a few minutes. Jennie turned her phone back on. It was a good thing she'd charged it in her car before they'd crashed. She still had 47 percent battery life. "I promised Trooper Carter I'd listen to messages daily."

Her phone buzzed several times. She ignored the social media notifications. She had three text messages, two from the trooper and one from Aiden. She responded to Aiden's first, telling him she was fine. Then she listened to Trooper Carter's messages. His first one made her nearly faint with relief. "They picked up the guy from my apartment building. His name is Zane. He's Steve's nephew."

Luke nodded. "That would explain why he was so willing to do his dirty work."

"Carter says they know he was the one who tried to break into my apartment through the window. Apparently, there are cameras in the halls, but none on the outside of the building."

She could never go back there. Not to live. Not after this.

The second message was far more menacing. She listened and then raised stricken eyes to Luke's face. "Steve Curtis has been spotted outside of Grove City. He's getting closer."

Luke placed his hands on her shoulders. "He doesn't know where you are. There are no cameras here. We'll stay on the grounds. There's always someone around."

She nodded. His words comforted her, but she couldn't shake the feeling of impending doom. Later that morning, she walked over to the side of the house. There was a lovely picturesque view. The land sloped down into a sort of steep, rocky cliff. It was isolated and peaceful at the same time.

It was the perfect place to pray. She closed her eyes, feeling as if she were in the midst of God's presence. She prayed for her son and Luke and for the rest of his family. When she opened her eyes, she was at peace.

She didn't have time to ponder for long. The next day would be Christmas morning. She didn't know if the Amish gave gifts or not. If so, she had nothing to give anyone. Not even LJ. That made her sadder than anything.

Christmas Day dawned bright, the blue sky and white snow the perfect setting for celebration. Jennie found a few minutes to pray in the little area she'd discovered the day before. The view of the area around her and the sky was breathtaking. After a few minutes, though, her peace was invaded with a strange sensation. The space between her shoulder blades tingled.

Was she being watched? She turned in all directions.

When she saw no one there, she shrugged but could not shake her anxious feeling. She strode from the spot, arms clasped tight around her stomach, determined to keep herself and LJ close to the house that day.

The family celebration surprised her. There were gifts. Each family member received one. When she and LJ each were given a small gift from Luke, she was touched. "I have nothing for you," she mourned.

He shrugged. "We only generally get one gift. I already have mine." It was true. His mother had made him a new shirt.

After breakfast was cleared, Jennie witnessed her first ever singing. It was a tradition she wished she could experience every Christmas. It seemed to be the perfect blend of worship and fellowship.

It was the best Christmas she'd ever had. Luke was at her side. Several times that day, their hands or shoulders had touched. Nothing dramatic. But little touches that filled her with warmth. She went to bed that night happier than she'd felt in a long time.

The next day, she woke, planning to spend the day helping Sarah in the kitchen. She made time to visit her little rocky cliff to pray. She stayed there for fifteen minutes, enjoying the peace, before the sense of being watched invaded her calm.

She set out to find Luke. "I think we're being watched."

Luke didn't tell her she was imagining things. He took Raymond and went to look around the area. She and LJ stayed near the barn.

LJ was enraptured with Buster. "She knows me, Mama. Daddy showed her how to find me by how I smell."

That was no small thing. And it also told her why they'd been so quick to give him a puppy. Luke was making sure he could protect them to the best of his ability.

When he came back, she relaxed.

"Nothing was there, Jennie. We'll keep watch. But for now, I think we're okay. Maybe stay in the *haus* today?"

She agreed and took LJ with her.

He was restless and complained. All he wanted to do was go play with Buster. But dogs were not allowed in the house. Theresa finally managed to convince him to go play a game.

"I'll keep him out of your way while you help *Mamm*."

For a moment, Jennie felt guilty. She was LJ's mother, after all. But LJ was feeling fractious, and he was happy with Theresa.

Jennie helped Sarah, and the older woman explained how Amish women spent their days. They made fresh bread from scratch and Sarah even showed her how to make a homemade pie crust. Jennie had never really cared for cooking, but suddenly she realized she loved to bake. It was a revelation to her.

When it was almost time for lunch, she went in search of LJ. He and Theresa had gone to play in the basement.

They weren't there. Jennie frowned. Where could they have gone?

She went upstairs. Anna was in the living room. "Anna, have you seen LJ?"

Anna pointed to the hook where the coats were kept. LJ's coat and Theresa's cloak were missing. "Outside. On the porch."

Her breath stopped. Theresa had taken him to play on the porch. Outside. In the open.

Dashing out the front door, Jennie ran around to the side of the porch. They weren't there. She raced down the steps and out onto the driveway, finally coming to a stop, terrified.

Theresa's black bonnet was lying on the ground. But there was no sign of the girl. Or of LJ.

The pit dropped out of Jennie's stomach. She knew that Theresa would never walk around outside without the bonnet. And she definitely would never leave it lying on the ground where a buggy could roll over it. Footsteps thudded on the porch behind her. "Jennie? What's going on? Anna told me you needed me."

Panicked, she turned to face Luke. She pointed at the bonnet on the ground. The chilling shimmer in his eyes told her he'd drawn the same conclusion she had.

LJ and Theresa were missing.

FIFTEEN

Jennie raced off the porch, her sides heaving as sobs shook her. She tried to call for LJ, but she was too distraught. She knew what kind of monster Steve was.

"Jennie!" Luke ran up beside her and grabbed her hand.

She turned to face him, her whole being quivering with terror. "Luke," she finally managed to sob out. "He has LJ and Theresa. I know he does! We have to find them!" Inside she was struggling not to give in to despair. There was still hope that they would find LJ on the property.

Luke leaned in and put his forehead briefly on hers. "Lord *Gott*, please, help us find our son."

A simple prayer, but one she felt deep down in her spirit. "Amen," she choked out.

"I'll go out back, search the pastures."

She nodded. "I'll look out front and in the side yard."

He squeezed her hand one final time, then he was off. His gate was uneven on the snow-covered lane, but Jennie didn't watch for long. She pivoted and ran, pumping her arms for additional speed. As she whipped around the corner of the house, her white *kapp* flew off her head. She didn't pause. LJ needed her.

He wasn't in the front yard. She ran between the tractor and the equipment, peering underneath everything. Nothing.

That left the side yard.

The yard that seemed so peaceful in the morning when she came out to pray now appeared desolate. In some ways, it even seemed to have a menacing edge—all the rocks, plunging down at such a sharp angle.

LJ wouldn't come out here, she told herself. He knew it wasn't a safe place, and she had told him often enough that he wasn't allowed here. He would not have disobeyed her.

But he was four. What four-year-old boy could resist the lure of the forbidden?

She stepped closer to the edge, peering down the cliff. At first, she didn't see anything. She almost left, relieved that he hadn't fallen down.

But something urged her to look again.

There. Beneath two slabs of rock, a sheet of paper jutted out. Her breath caught sharply when she saw her name printed in large blocky letters on the top of the page.

Someone knew she was here.

Edging down the slope a couple feet, she slipped on the icy terrain and caught herself on her hands. They stung where the skin was scraped off. She ignored the pain. Reaching the paper, she pulled it out from between the rocks. When she climbed up to the top, she opened the folded sheet, vaguely aware of the blood from her hands smearing the page.

Jennie. Such a pretty place you've found to walk in the mornings. I like watching you.

She shivered, remembering the feeling that someone had been there. Oh, why had she ignored that? Just because she hadn't seen anyone! A tear slipped out of her eye. She brushed it away with angry fingers.

I have your little boy and the girl. Cute little thing. He's not hurt. Yet. If you want him to stay that way, you will do exactly what I say.

Ditch the Amish people you're with. Come down to the end of the drive and follow the bike path across the road. If you bring your friends with you, your son and your friend will pay for your disobedience.

There was no signature, but it didn't matter. She knew exactly who had sent it. Steve. No one else would want her dead this badly.

She had no choice. How she wished she had one last chance to see Luke. She had no doubt Steve would kill her. But maybe Luke could still find LJ and Theresa. If Steve released them.

Carefully, she bent and placed the letter under a rock on the dirt portion of the driveway, leaving it so it wouldn't blow away, but neither would it be hard to see.

Following the directions, she strode down the lane, looking behind her to make sure no one was following. She didn't want Luke to find she was gone, not yet. If he did, she didn't know what would happen to LJ or Luke's sister. Their safety had to be her first and only priority.

When she crossed the road, she found the neglected bike path. None of the Amish in the area would have used it. Luke had told her once a long time ago that their bishop didn't let them ride bikes or anything with rubber wheels. The path grew dimmer with each step she took under the overgrown trees.

A movement to her left startled her. With a small shriek, she spun, her hand flying to cover her heart.

Brenda, the clerk from the bank, emerged from the trees, a cold smile on her face.

"Brenda?" Jennie gasped. The idea that she could be involved in something so heinous was unbelievable.

The other woman laughed, a sound that scraped against Jennie's raw nerves. It was a bitter, angry sound. "You have been more trouble than you're worth. The tracking device under your car was supposed to make you easy to find. But then you left your car behind. It's taken too much time finding you again." Brenda tossed her head, her eyes narrowing to slits. Jennie was reminded of a snake. "If you'd died like you were supposed to, none of this would have happened."

Jennie's head swam, unable to process what was happening. "But why? I never knew you until I moved to Meadville, did I? What did I ever do to you?"

Brenda grabbed her arm, shoving Jennie in front of her and forcing her to walk. "To me? Nothing. But to Steve, plenty."

"How do you know Steve?"

"Keep moving," Brenda snapped when Jennie's steps slowed. "I wrote to him in prison. We fell in love. He told me how you framed him, how you had schemed against him."

Jennie had heard of women falling for men who were in prison before. She'd never put much credence to such stories before. Now she knew better. "I didn't—"

Brenda gave her arm a fierce yank. Jennie cried out in pain. "I don't want to hear your lies. If Morgan hadn't screwed up, you'd be gone and I could start my life with Steve. Now I have to wait until you're taken care of."

Jennie tried to keep up. Morgan. Randi's brother. The one who'd been stalking her on Steve's orders.

"Morgan's dead."

Brenda laughed. It reminded Jennie of a coyote howling, hungry and without mercy. She shivered. When Brenda laughed again, Jennie knew her fear amused the other woman. "You didn't think we could let him live, not after he almost destroyed everything we'd worked so hard for?"

"Steve killed him? His own friend?"

Now Brenda snorted. "Morgan Griggs was nothing to Steve. How could he be? Nothing but a low-life loser. I actually enjoyed pulling the trigger."

"You!" Jennie tripped in her shock.

"Keep going," Brenda snarled in her ear. "I'd love to shoot you right here, but Steve wants that pleasure for himself."

Jennie's hands and feet were becoming numb from the cold. Her heart felt like a frozen lump of rock sitting in the middle of her chest. She'd been so wrong about Brenda.

How blind had she been to never see the net Steve had put in place, closing in around her? Morgan. Brenda. Zane. All people she'd known but hadn't really paid any attention to. Had there been any others?

If she ever got out of this mess, how would she go back to her life? The idea of raising a child in that world filled her with horror.

If Luke found her message and managed to rescue LJ and Theresa, at least she would know that her baby would grow up in a world that valued life and honored God.

Brenda led her down the path to a waiting car, engine running. She slipped handcuffs on Jennie's wrists and forced her onto the back floorboard. Jennie scrunched into the small space, her back twisted funny.

Leaning her head against the back door, she closed her eyes. There was no way out for her. Not right now. She'd have to keep watch to seize her opportunity.

She could pray. With silent tears running down her cheeks, she begged God to protect her family. To spare LJ and Theresa, and to protect Luke as he came after them. Lastly, she pleaded that God would send someone to save them all.

Exhaustion overtook her. When she awoke, the car was stopped. Where were they?

She tried to see through the opposite window, but all she could see was sky.

The door she was leaning on opened. She was grabbed from behind and dragged roughly from the car. When she was on her feet, she was spun around to come face-to-face with the man who had haunted her dreams for years.

"Well, if it isn't my darling stepdaughter," Steve snarled, his breath hitting her face. She blinked and pulled back. He chuckled. She shivered. "I've been waiting a long time to meet up with you again."

"LJ!" Luke shouted his son's name as he tore into the barn. His son loved the animals. Maybe Theresa had taken him in to see the new puppies. He found the animals in the back with their mother, but there was no sign of his son. Or his little sister.

If he lost either of them…

He wouldn't go there.

"Luke, did you find them?"

Raymond and Simon bolted into the barn.

"*Nee*, not yet. Help me search."

Without a word, both brothers took off in different directions, one searching the fields, the other heading into the woods. Luke was grateful for the assistance. His *daed* met him in the yard. "Your *mamm* went to the neighbors' *haus* to ask for help. What can I do?"

Luke clapped a hand on his *daed*'s shoulder and blinked the moisture from his eyes. "Help me search. And pray, *Daed*."

"Always."

The men fanned out and continued to call for LJ and Theresa. There was no response. A lead ball settled in Luke's gut. If Theresa heard him, she'd respond if she could. He checked the shop, although he doubted his son would disobey and go in there. And he knew that his sister would never take him in there. She knew that their *daed* had dangerous tools and equipment there. It was no place for a child. LJ had been warned not to venture inside without an adult, and up to now, had never once tried to test the rule.

It was colder now than it had been when Luke had first run outside. The sky would be growing dark soon. Maybe Jennie had found them. He hoped and prayed it was so as he dashed to the side of the *haus*. Rounding the corner of porch, he halted, confused. Jennie's *kapp* was near the base of the stairs. He picked it up and shoved it in his pocket.

Jennie, however, wasn't there. Had she already headed inside? If she had found LJ, she would have come to let him know. Or she would have sent Theresa to him. He knew that she wouldn't leave him searching in suspense. So where had she gone?

A chill fell over him as he looked at the slippery rocks near the top of the incline. Jennie loved this area. Maybe she'd gotten too close and fallen down. Dread bloomed in him as an image of his beautiful Jennie lying injured at the bottom of the rocks popped into his brain. *No!*

Running to the edge, he looked down, nearly falling to his knees when he looked clear to the bottom and saw neither Jennie nor LJ lying there. He frowned. But where had she gone? He started to turn away.

A flutter on the driveway caught his attention. A paper was stuck under a rock. The way it was positioned, he knew someone had left it there on purpose. When he moved closer, he saw Jennie's name on it. As he bent, he saw the red smears. Blood.

His throat closed. Grabbing the note, he read it over, then read it again, horror freezing his veins. He knew exactly what had happened. Steve had kidnapped his son and his sister, and his brave Jennie had gone as a sacrifice to save them.

But she'd left the note for him, so clearly she expected him to come to her rescue. Jennie wasn't one to run toward danger if she had any choice.

Clenching the paper in his hands, he bellowed for his brothers and his *daed*. His *daed* arrived first, dragging in huge gasping breaths. He must have run all the way. The thunder of approaching footsteps alerted him to his brothers rounding the corner.

"Jennie's stepfather has them both, and now he has Jennie, too."

Raymond took the letter from him and read it out loud for everyone's benefit. Hearing the words again sent daggers of fear and agony shooting through Luke's heart. His spirit cried out to *Gott*, begging Him to have mercy on them and protect his family.

"We have to contact the police," Simon stated. "It's the only way we can do this."

Luke knew his brother was right. He chafed against the time that would be wasted waiting for the police to arrive. But there was nothing he could do against those who didn't blink at the thought of killing others.

He ran to the phone in the workshop and dialed 911. The operator assured him that a police vehicle was en route and would arrive within the next ten minutes.

Ten minutes. It seemed an eternity to wait while his family was in mortal danger.

He snatched up the leash for Buster.

"What are you doing?" Raymond latched onto his arm. Luke shook him off.

"*Ach*, you know what I'm doing. I'm going after my wife and child. The police won't let me come, but I can't stay back. Buster will be able to find LJ. Give them the note."

Without waiting for a response, he ran to the *haus* and grabbed the shirt LJ had worn the day before. Racing from the *haus*, he burst into the garage and attached the leash to the dog.

"Come on, girl. Let's go get LJ."

The dog woofed as if she understood what he was saying, though it was probably wishful thinking. Luke let her sniff the shirt. With a growl, the pup started sniffing the ground. When she moved, she pulled Luke toward the forgotten bike path across the road.

Luke followed the pup down the path. His other hand was clenched tightly around Jennie's *kapp*. It was his one link to her now. *Please, Gott, lead me to her.*

It was going to be dark soon. He arrived at the end of the trail. There was no sign of Jennie, LJ or Theresa. Buster whined. He patted her head.

Discouraged, he went home. The police had arrived. It was a strange sight to see their vehicles in his drive, lights flashing. The neighbors across the road were huddled on their porch, whispering together.

He barely registered them, his mind mired in his grief and anxiety.

Thankfully, the troopers didn't lecture him about going after Jennie.

"We've put out a BOLO," the trooper in charge informed him. When Luke stared at him, he explained, "That means Be On the Lookout. We've released pictures of Jennie and LJ from Jennie's Facebook page, as well as a picture of Steve Curtis. The hope is someone will see them and call in."

Luke swallowed, trying to dislodge the lump in his throat. "What do we do while we're waiting?" He didn't dare ask what happened if no one called in. The idea that he might lose three people so dear to him at once was overwhelming.

"Easy, son." The trooper placed a hand on his shoulder. "I know you're anxious. We're going to do everything possible to find your loved ones. Right now, we're going to organize a search of the area. Gather all your neighbors. There's a chance that the kidnappers are still in the area."

"What if we see something?"

"Don't, I repeat, do not under any circumstance approach. Steve Curtis is dangerous. It will help no one if one of you get yourselves killed."

The trooper gave him a pointed glance. Apparently, he had decided that if anyone would act rashly, it would be Luke. Luke refrained from voicing the retort that hovered on his tongue. Sparring with the police wouldn't help them find his family.

For the next hour, the neighbors searched the area. Unusual tracks had been spotted past the bike trail. Someone had driven a car back there. Luke knew in his heart it had been Jennie's kidnapper.

A call came in on the police radio. Someone had spotted a man who fit Steve Curtis's description. Luke held his breath as the police gathered around.

"There's a possible sighting of the suspect at the abandoned Schwartz barn, three miles outside of town."

"That's hard to reach," one of the troopers called out. "The bridge is out."

"There's a back way," Luke burst out, interrupting the conversation. "The Amish use the road all the time. We can show you the way."

The chief scowled, his brow furrowed in thought. Luke hoped he wouldn't tell him to stand back now, not after letting him and the neighbors join in the search. When the trooper's gaze landed on him, Luke suspected that the man already knew Luke wouldn't stay home. He was going to search for his family, whether the police wanted him to or not.

"Fine," the man bit out. "Let's hurry, though."

Luke ran to the cruiser and got in before the trooper could change his mind. Soon they were on their way. Luke wanted to tell the trooper to speed up, but bit his tongue. If the situation hadn't been so serious, he might have enjoyed the irony that he was the one who wanted the *Englisch* man to go faster.

As it was, he was struggling to hold on to his hope

with all the strength of his soul. He prayed for all he was worth that Jennie, LJ and Theresa were alive and would be safe.

Hold on, Jennie. I'm coming to get you.

SIXTEEN

Luke clenched his fists as the cruiser bounced along the back road. It was littered with potholes, and Luke guessed that the car managed to hit every single one.

He was glad he was wearing his hat. It gave him a little extra padding whenever his head hit the roof as they bounced along. Not much, but some. The detour around the bridge added ten minutes to their trip. When his teeth began hurting, Luke realized that he was grinding his molars together in his frustration.

He should pray. He knew it, but his mind was a mass of confusion. His usual clarity and focus had disappeared with Jennie, LJ and Theresa.

Gott, help them.

Mentally, he prayed the words over and over, a litany to God straight from his aching heart. He had to trust that God would hear and answer his prayers.

"We're nearing the road," Luke pointed out. "That one on the right will take you around the back of the Schwartz property. There's a smaller bridge. Only one vehicle can cross it at a time."

"Got it." The trooper glanced at him out of the corner of his eye. "I'm not going to turn on lights or sirens.

If I go in hot, it will announce our presence and we'll lose any advantage we might have."

"*Jah*, I understand."

When they arrived at the bridge, Luke had to bite his tongue to keep from exclaiming while a truck with a long trailer crossed over. The trailer was wobbly, and Luke feared it would jackknife, blocking their only route to Jennie and LJ for hours, or at least until they managed to clear it.

Finally, the truck and trailer cleared the bridge. Luke let out his breath. The cruiser wound around the back of the property.

"We're going to park it here," the trooper announced. "From here we go on foot."

Luke followed him toward the barn. Raymond and Simon joined them, startling Luke. He hadn't realized that his family had been following them, though it shouldn't have surprised him. He'd been so focused on Jennie and LJ, he hadn't stopped to consider what everyone else would be doing.

It seemed like everyone was moving in slow motion. He wanted to burst through the door of the barn. He couldn't, he knew. One rash move could get Jennie, LJ or Theresa killed. It was difficult, but he had to trust that *Gott* would work through the troopers who were now spanning out around the building.

He'd never seen anyone move so silently. Nor had he seen such a coordinated effort. One motion from the chief, and the troopers efficiently moved to do his bidding. Luke didn't approve of guns, but he was impressed with the precision of the operation.

The chief waved, and a small group entered the barn from the back. Luke moved in closer to the window, close enough to see what was happening. His heart nearly stopped when he saw his sister sitting against the wall, a large bruise on her forehead. Otherwise she appeared to be safe. In her arms she held his son. LJ was clinging tightly to his aunt. She probably couldn't have set him down if she wanted to.

Jennie stood in the center of the floor. Steve Curtis circled around her, his venomous smile telling Luke that he had no intention of letting her walk out of that barn alive.

What Luke hadn't expected was to see the teller from the bank, leaning against the wall.

The window was broken. They could hear the voices from inside the barn. Luke stood as still as he could to avoid drawing their attention. When the chief started to edge away from the window, Luke took the cue and followed. He'd do whatever he was told if it meant keeping his family alive.

Jennie's skin crawled as Steve continued to march a path around her. What was he waiting for? Would he let her son go free, like he promised?

"Your note said you'd free the others if I came."

Steve laughed. It was a sound totally devoid of either humor or humanity. "I lied. Why would I set them free when having them here hurts you? Don't you know I've dreamed of this moment for years? When I figured out where you were, it wasn't hard to find spies to keep an eye on you. That's how I learned that your husband hadn't really died. Once I knew that, it wasn't hard to figure out where his family lived."

Jennie had been so blind. She'd thought that Pete had been watching her. It never occurred to her that it might have been Brenda or the tenant in the downstairs apartment. Now Zane was on his way to prison and Morgan was dead. If help didn't arrive, Brenda and Steve might make it out of here.

"Come on, Steve. I brought her to you. Can you just finish this so we can leave?" Brenda cast a glare around her. "This place gives me the creeps. All these spiderwebs. And the smell! I shudder to think what that could be."

Steve ignored her and continued to try to bait Jennie.

Jennie shivered when Brenda looked at her. Those eyes were stone-cold. The eyes of a killer. How had she not seen it?

Brenda stalked in closer. She stopped a few feet away from them, arms crossed over her chest. "I want to go, Steve. I don't like it here." She flicked a glare at Jennie.

Steve sneered. "Then go, already. I'm not ready to leave yet. I've waited years for this moment, and I intend to enjoy it."

Shock was followed by anger on Brenda's face. "What do you mean, I can leave? We're a team on this. We're getting married."

Jennie stared when Steve let out what could only be called a snicker. "Not likely."

Brenda went pale. Fury washed all the beauty from her face. "Not likely? Want to explain that, Steve dear?"

Was the man an idiot? Couldn't he hear the deadly intent in her voice?

When he switched his attention to Brenda, Jennie moved back, away from them. She couldn't leave, not with her son and Theresa in harm's way. But she knew the look of a woman about ready to explode. She also saw the flash of steel in Brenda's waistband. There was not a doubt in her mind that the woman was capable of using it.

"I have no intention of marrying you," Steve was saying, "now or ever. Go ahead and leave. I don't care. You've served your purpose and brought Jennie to me. I have no more need of you."

"Steve! I love you!"

Steve snarled at her. "Well, I don't love you. Do you understand? You were a tool to get me what I wanted, but I don't need you anymore. I definitely have no plans to saddle myself with your whining. It's driving me crazy."

Jennie dove for the floor when Brenda whipped out the gun. The sudden blast reverberated through the barn. LJ screamed, the sound quickly muffled when Theresa hugged him.

Steve landed with a thud next to Jennie, a cloud of dust rising around him. She scuttled away from him, then stopped as Brenda moved to stand over her. She looked up into the face of death.

"I guess I didn't have to wait to shoot you, after all," Brenda said. Tears tracked down her face. "I killed him and it's all your fault." She raised the gun again.

Before she could shoot, the door swung open and a trooper charged inside, knocking the gun from her hand. Within seconds Brenda was in handcuffs and being led away as an officer read her her rights.

Luke was at Jennie's side. "Jennie? Are you hurt?"

She shook her head. "No. You came."

When he folded her in his arms, she didn't protest, just sank against his warmth, treasuring the kisses he planted on her head. LJ ran to them, screaming their names. She looked up to see Simon and Raymond hugging Theresa.

All was well.

* * *

Jennie had trouble wrapping her mind around it. After so many years of living in fear that Steve Curtis would come after her, the man who had haunted her nightmares was dead. She stared at his body as the coroner confirmed his death and the paramedics covered him with a dark blanket. She half expected him to open his eyes, sit up and start spewing insults.

Instead, his form remained still. The paramedics lifted him onto a stretcher and placed him in the back of the coroner's SUV. When the doors were shut and the vehicle pulled away, she began to shake.

"Jennie?" Luke sat beside her, his face, so dear to her, somber. She couldn't understand the bleakness she saw in his eyes. They were free. Steve was gone.

"He's dead, Luke. You saved us."

He cracked a smile. There was no humor in it. It was the saddest excuse for a smile she'd ever seen. "Well, I had a lot of help saving you."

What was she missing?

"Ma'am, are you sure you don't want to go to the hospital?" She turned to see a young paramedic. "I really think we need to bring you in and get you checked out."

She was ready to protest. The hospital was not where she wanted to go.

"Your son needs checked out, as well."

All protests died on her lips. She wouldn't skimp on treatment for LJ.

Luke stood.

Panic hit her. He was leaving. She knew he was. She couldn't let him go. They needed to talk. He needed to understand that she loved him. She and LJ needed him in their lives, and she'd do what was necessary to make that happen.

Even if it meant becoming Amish. Because now she understood. God wanted them together. There was a reason that Luke had met her so many years ago. Going back to her old world no longer appealed.

If only she could convince him of that.

"Luke, come with me to the hospital."

His gaze flinched away from hers. She pleaded with him silently to not shut her out. Finally, he responded, "I will drive over in my buggy."

Before she could argue, he was gone. She was soon lost in the flurry of activity that followed. She and LJ were loaded into the ambulance.

"What happened to Theresa?" she asked the paramedic who climbed in back with them. "You know, the young Amish girl who was rescued with us."

The paramedic nodded. "I know who you mean. She was only slightly bruised and shaken up. She declined treatment."

Vaguely, Jennie wondered if Theresa's father had declined for her, but rejected that idea. Luke's parents were warm and gentle-hearted people. She knew that they only wanted what was best for their children. Her eyes slid over to where LJ lay sound asleep on the stretcher beside her. Just as she wanted what was best for her son.

"Can someone call my brother for me?" she blurted. The need to hear her older brother's calm voice welled up inside. Aiden would help her sort things out. Without judgment.

At the hospital, Jennie and LJ were wheeled inside and a series of tests followed. It took several hours, but both were declared out of danger. "We're letting you go," the emergency room doctor told her. "We need these beds for people who actually need them."

When he grinned, she knew he was teasing her.

Still no Luke.

Disappointment bubbled up inside her when she realized that Luke had no intention of stopping by to see her. She knew he was drawing back, but she never would have expected that. What about his son? Regardless of Luke's feelings for her, she knew he loved his son.

He loved her, too, she thought desperately. She knew he did. He just couldn't or wouldn't admit it.

She was holding in the tears when she and LJ were wheeled out past the emergency room doors to the lobby area. The small area next to the reception desk was filled with a dozen chairs, most of them occupied by patients waiting for their turn to be seen in the emergency room.

Don't lose control here, she warned herself. *There are too many people watching.*

The hospital doors whooshed open. A familiar face strode in, his face daring anyone to get in his way.

Aiden.

Seeing her brother, her control fled. Sobbing, Jennie held out her arms and found herself engulfed in a bear hug. Over his shoulder, she saw LJ was receiving the same treatment from his aunt Sophie. Closing her eyes, Jennie allowed herself to be a small girl again, crying on her brother's shoulder as he comforted her.

When she was finally in control again, she leaned back. Aiden released her, but he didn't completely let go.

"What happened, kid? The last time I talked to you, you were fine. Then I get a call that you and my nephew are in the hospital, and here you are dressed like the Amish. Speak to me."

"It was Steve, Aiden."

At the name of their monstrous stepfather, Aiden's face went still, his eyes granite hard. "Where is he?"

"He's dead." Relief leaked into the words. She'd never be thankful for another person's death but knowing that she was free from Steve brought some semblance of peace. "And, Aiden, my husband, Luke—he's alive."

Aiden's jaw dropped. She wanted to giggle at his expression but bit her lip instead. She didn't want him to think that she was hysterical.

"Alive? How is that possible?" His jaw tensed. "Did he abandon you? Did he—"

She put her hand over his mouth to silence him. "Nothing like that. He was in an accident and lost his memory. It's true," she hurried to assure him when his lip curled into a sneer of disbelief.

"So where is this husband of yours?"

Good question. She peered over his shoulder and saw an Amish buggy pulling into the drive. She recognized Luke and Raymond. Luke hopped down from the buggy, while Raymond stayed outside.

"He's on his way. Look, do you think you could take LJ somewhere? Maybe go get him something to eat? I need to talk with Luke alone, and I'm not sure how this chat will end."

Aiden and Sophie exchanged glances. Aiden didn't want to go, Jennie could tell. But Sophie nodded. "We'll leave you two to sort things out. Here's my cell phone…" She handed the phone to Jennie. "Use it if you need us."

Gratefully, Jennie took the phone, wishing she had a pocket to put it in.

Aiden gave her one last hug and then swung LJ up onto his shoulders. "Come on, cowboy. How about we go and get us some grub?"

"Pizza!" LJ hollered, his fear replaced by the excitement of eating his favorite food with his uncle. "I want pizza. And root beer!"

He'd never get that at home. Root beer was a very special treat.

"You got it."

Aiden and Sophie left. As they walked out, they passed Luke. Aiden gave him a sharp once-over, then glanced back at Jennie, his head nodding toward Luke in question. He'd already figured out that her wearing an Amish dress meant her husband was Amish, too. She signed back, "Yes, that's him. I'll explain later."

She knew he'd understand. They'd both learned some sign language to talk with Celine since Aiden had married Sophie.

If he responded, she missed it. All of her attention was on the man moving her way, his expression solemn. This didn't bode well for their future.

"Is there anywhere we can talk?" he asked.

"Let's go to the cafeteria." It was far more public than she'd have liked, but it was the only place they could sit down without being under the gaze of the guards or other patients. This conversation might be the most devastating one she'd had in her short life.

Jennie ordered a cup of coffee and added two creams and two sugar packets before joining Luke at a table in the corner. She ordered it more to give herself something to keep her hands busy with than because she was actually thirsty. Her nerves were getting the better of her.

"Luke," she started, but then she stopped. What should she say? How could she convince him that they belonged together? His face was shuttered. There was a hopelessness in his expression that told her he'd already given up on them.

His next words confirmed it. "Jennie. You can go home now without fear, ain't so? Your stepfather and all those he hired are either dead or on their way to jail."

She braced herself. "But what if I don't want to go home? What if I want me and LJ to stay with you?"

Pain flashed across his eyes, leaving them shadowed and somehow hollow. "*Nee*, you can't, Jennie. I wish you could. But you're *Englisch* and have no place in my world."

Fear tickled her throat. She had to make him see!

"But what if I wasn't? *Englisch*, I mean." She leaned toward him as he started to shake his head, discarding her idea. "I'm serious, Luke. We could join your church, become Amish. I've seen the way you live, and I'm not scared of it."

"You've seen it for a few days. *Nee*, Jennie. You don't know what you're asking. Imagine weeks, months, years of living off the land, no technology. You'd be giving up modern conveniences, and what about Aiden?"

She blinked. "What about Aiden?"

"You'd not be able to contact him as often as you'd like. I can't stand the thought that you'd learn to despise me, and the life you chose. Once you become Amish, you can't leave. To do so would be to separate yourself from everything, even family. This way, I can still see LJ from time to time. He could get to know his grandparents."

He stood. "I wish you well."

He turned away, but then, as if he couldn't help himself, he spun back and walked to her. Bending down, he gave her a quick kiss, nothing more than a chaste brush of his lips against hers.

It was a kiss goodbye. Wordlessly, he strode out of the cafeteria, leaving her behind, tears stinging in her eyes while her heart quietly shattered in her chest.

SEVENTEEN

"You're not happy."

Luke avoided Raymond's eyes and shrugged, continuing to sand the table he'd been working on. Six days ago, he'd enjoyed the happiest Christmas he could remember, only to lose everything the next day. He'd done his best to pretend to be content with his life for the past five days since he left Jennie at the hospital. But every day, he got up with Jennie's face in front of his eyes. And soon after that, the image of LJ always followed. Luke's whole life had narrowed down to those two people, and he'd walked away from them as if they weren't the very beat of his heart.

It was a lie, but one he was helpless to change.

"Luke, look at me."

Unable to avoid his brother any longer, he held in a sigh and put the sander down before turning to meet the concerned gaze of his younger sibling.

"What do you want me to say, Ray?"

Raymond's brow furrowed. "*Ach*, I don't know. I want to see you smile. You haven't done so since you returned from the hospital."

Luke shrugged. It was true. But he hadn't felt like

smiling much. The only thing that kept him from total despair was knowing that whatever he was suffering through, *Gott* was with him. And he knew that Jennie wouldn't keep him from seeing LJ. Although his heart would shatter a bit more inside his chest every time he saw her. Whether she was Amish or not, in his heart, she was still his wife, the woman that he loved.

How did you get past that?

"I haven't felt like smiling. I'll be fine. I need some time."

"It's her, ain't so? It's Jennie."

A small spurt of anger shot up inside him. He smothered it. His brother meant no harm; he was concerned, that was all.

"*Jah*, it's Jennie. She's my wife, and the mother of my *kind*. I love her. I love them both, and I miss them."

Raymond nodded and rubbed his chin. His eyes got that faraway look that meant he was considering his words, planning how to say what was on his mind. "Does she love you?"

"*Jah*. She didn't say the words, but I know she does." Why else would she tell him she'd join his church? His way of life?

"Have you ever considered asking her to become Plain? If she joined the church, there'd be no obstacles."

It so closely mirrored what he had been thinking, for a moment Luke stared at his brother. "*Nee*, I have not asked her. How can I? It's not an easy life." He paused. "She offered, but I—"

Raymond's eyes bulged. "Your woman, your *wife*, offered to join the church, and you said *nee*?" If he'd been *Englisch*, he would have probably told Luke he was crazy.

Was he? Why had he shut her down so fast?

"What if she went through the classes and decided it wasn't for her?" Luke asked. Could he go through that pain?

"*Jah*, that's possible. Then you would know for sure, *jah*? But if you don't let her take that step, neither of you will ever know. You'll be alone your whole life, and your son will grow up outside of your *haus*."

Luke straightened and clenched his fists. "I never gave her a chance." A sense of certainty poured through him. "I need to go to her."

"*Jah*, you do. Should I come with you?"

"*Nee*." Luke shook his head, already striding toward the phone. "This is a trip I need to make alone. I don't know how long I will be gone."

"I will explain to *Mamm* and *Daed* for you."

Luke was already picking up the phone to call a driver. He nodded to let Raymond know he'd heard him. Now that he had a purpose, he didn't want to waste any more time. He was fortunate.

"Hey, Luke. I had a cancellation just twenty minutes ago. I can be at your house in forty minutes," the driver said.

He felt he'd received a confirmation that he was on the correct path. *Danke, Gott.*

This time Luke wouldn't let fear or his own doubts get in the way. Hanging up the phone, he strode briskly to the *haus*. He would have run, but the last thing he needed now was to fall on the ice and break his leg again. He smiled at the thought, his first smile in a week.

His *mamm* called after him as he came inside and

took the stairs two at a time. At the top of the stairs, he turned to look back.

"Go," Raymond ordered. "I'll explain."

Luke didn't wait to hear more. He had packing to do. His pulse was thrumming through his veins. Soon, he'd see his Jennie. Was she still his? Had she changed her mind in the week they'd been apart?

When Sam arrived, Luke was ready for him.

"Happy New Year, Luke."

Luke blinked. It was New Year's Eve. He'd totally lost track of the time in his misery. One day had blended into the next since he'd left Jennie at the hospital. Wow.

"I hope it will be, Sam. Same to you."

As they drove closer to Meadville, the muscles in his shoulders grew taut. He wouldn't let himself think of what would happen if she told him to go. He wouldn't blame her; he'd done that very thing when he'd turned down her offer to become Amish.

How arrogant he'd been! He'd never given her a chance. Nor had he asked *Gott* if that was His will.

When Sam pulled up in front of her apartment, Luke's heart was pounding in his ears. He forced himself to get out of the van to meet his fate. He laughed at the thought, but the laugh was shaky.

There were voices inside Jennie's apartment. He almost turned around, but instead he steeled himself and rapped his knuckles against the door. When it opened, he found himself speechless as he stared into the eyes that had haunted him for the past week.

"Luke." Those beautiful brown eyes were swimming in tears. Or was it his own eyes?

It was both.

"Jennie. Can we talk?"

She hesitated, then nodded. Swinging the door open, she gestured for him to enter. "Come meet my brother first."

Aiden Forster looked at him with suspicion, but then, what protective older brother wouldn't? Sophie Forster, however, looked between Luke and Jennie, and her face broke open wide in a smile.

"Finally," was all she said.

Celine waved at him. She looked like a younger version of Sophie.

Jennie looked unsure for a moment, glancing around the apartment.

Sophie came to the rescue. "Go. Have your talk. Figure things out. We'll stay here with LJ."

"Let me get my coat," Jennie told him. He nodded.

As they left the apartment, he wanted to take her hand in his. Jennie, however, shoved both hands in her coat pockets. He could feel the distance she was placing between them, and not just physically.

He knew she was protecting herself, but inside he was struggling to hold his growing anxiety at bay.

Outside, Sam was still waiting.

Luke moved to the van. "Sam, could you drive us to the Diamond?"

In the center of Meadville was a large oval-shaped town square, roughly the size of a city block. Traffic flowed around a gazebo and a fountain standing in the very center, perfect for a private conversation.

"Sure thing."

Luke held open the back door so Jennie could climb in, then he followed her. She might be silent, but he wouldn't deny himself the pleasure of sitting near her. When he inhaled, the soft fragrance that was uniquely

Jennie drifted past his nostrils. It soothed his anxiety to a small extent. He was with her and she had agreed to talk with him.

That was hopeful.

Ten minutes later, Sam pulled into one of the parking spaces that surrounded the Diamond.

Silently, they stepped out of the vehicle. Luke grabbed on to her hand before she could put it in her pocket. To his delight, she didn't protest. His heart warmed as her slender fingers wrapped around his hand. Together they walked toward the gazebo. In its center stood a huge decorated Christmas tree. As they drew closer, their faces were bathed in the light emanating from the bulbs.

"It's so pretty."

He glanced at her. "*Jah.* Beautiful."

She met his eyes and blushed. "I meant the tree, silly."

"I didn't."

A smile tugged at the corners of her mouth. Encouraged, he squeezed her hand. "Let's go sit in the gazebo. We can talk privately there."

Luke tugged on her hand. Jennie followed him up the steps of the gazebo. Up close, the Christmas tree was breathtaking, shining and shimmering with silver tinsel and hundreds of colored lights. The tree was so round and fluffy that when Luke led her to the bench on the inside wall, she could still almost touch the branches.

She watched as Luke lowered himself cautiously at her side. Not too close. Their knees barely grazed each other. Still, she felt her pulse kick up at his nearness. Their breath misted and mingled in the air.

She waited. Should she say anything? Something to get the conversation rolling? Her mind, usually so quick with a sharp comment, was a complete blank.

"Jennie…"

She leaned forward, silently encouraging him to continue. He glanced at her and smiled. Her breath caught at the tenderness in his gaze. At the wealth of love and caring she saw.

Was she dreaming? No. Her heart recognized that emotion. He did love her.

"Were you serious," he finally asked, his voice husky with emotion, "when you said you'd be willing to become Amish?"

She blinked against the sudden tears. Her happy-ever-after was so close. *Please, Lord, if it's Your will. Please.* She couldn't even form her entire desire, but that was okay. God knew her heart. She could trust in that now.

Luke was starting to look concerned. Oh, she needed to respond. Clearing her throat, she nodded. "I was serious. I have thought about it. There's nothing for me in the *Englisch* world. God gave me a husband, and He gave me a son. I want to be where we can all be together, as a family."

His brows drew together. "It's not an easy life. Amish women work very hard, and there would be no technology."

The skills she'd worked so hard to acquire would not help her if she became Amish. It touched her that he understood that and was anxious not to take it away from her if it was important. It wasn't.

"I don't care. Luke, my career was a way to feed my son and to pay my rent. It was never something I loved. It was something I was good at, but it brought me no joy. Not really. And I did find joy in helping your mother with the simple work she does. More than that, it was fulfilling, to know that my work directly benefited my family."

He grinned at her. It was a bit wobbly, but still a grin.

"We wouldn't be able to live as husband and wife, not at first. You'd have to go through classes with the bishop. He'd want to make sure that you were making an informed decision, one you could live with for the rest of your life. It's no small thing, leaving the *Englisch* world behind."

"I understand." She hesitated. There was one point that made her pause. "What about my brother? Would I be separated from Aiden and his family?" She had lived so many years without her older brother, she didn't want to lose him again. She held her breath, waiting for his answer.

"*Nee*, I don't think so."

She let out the breath in a puff of mist. For a second, his face was obscured until it dissipated. "I was worried about that."

"*Jah*, I can see that. We live apart from the *Englisch*, but they are still our friends. You would still be able to write them and have them visit."

She could deal with that. "Then, yes, I want to go through the classes and join the Amish church. I want to be your wife again."

He leaned down and kissed her forehead. "I believe with all my heart that it wouldn't have made a difference if my memories had never returned. I was already falling in love with you all over again."

She knew how that felt.

"I fell in love with you when we were teenagers. When you came back into my life, I didn't know the man you'd become. You were so much more serious, and so dedicated to your faith and family. At first, I resented that, because your memory loss had taken you from me. And as I got to know you, I realized I was falling in love with you again. And it scared me because I knew that there were barriers that blocked our being together."

"I felt that, too. I didn't see how we could make it work. I couldn't ask you to join the church. It would be too much. Or I thought it would. I prayed to *Gott*, leaving it in His hands, if He wanted us to be together."

She leaned in and placed a gentle kiss on his cheek, the barest touch of her lips to his cold skin. Her lips tingled. "I think we have His answer. He wants us to be a family again."

"Should we tell our son?"

She nodded, her heart overflowing with joy and affection for the man beside her.

LJ, of course, was thrilled with the idea of his parents getting back together. "I'll get to live with both of you? All the time?" he demanded, his little hands on his hips.

"All the time," she promised.

"Goody!" LJ bounded forward to hug both his parents. "And *Grossmammi* Beiler? *Grossdawdi* Beiler?"

"Well." Luke rustled his hair. "We won't live with your grandparents. But you'll see them often. Which means you'll get lots of cookies."

Aiden moved to hug his sister. "Are you sure, Jennie?"

She appreciated his concern. "I'm sure, Aiden. I've loved him for so long. We belong together."

Sophie swooped in to kiss both their cheeks, and Sophie's sister, Celine, hugged her tight. She moved back to sign, "I love you, Aunt Jennie."

"Love you back," Jennie signed.

Soon after that, Aiden and Sophie gathered up their things, Celine and their daughter, and left. Rose was asleep on Aiden's shoulder as Jennie shut the door gently behind them.

Luke and Jennie put LJ to bed together. Because that was important to a little boy. Jennie was sure that he would be awake for hours, he was so hyper. She was wrong. Within twenty minutes, he was sound asleep.

After LJ went to bed, Luke and Jennie stayed up talking. They talked about everything from where they would live to their hope that they'd be blessed with a large family.

"I only had Aiden," she confided. "I'd love for LJ to be surrounded with siblings."

"He will also have many cousins." Luke grabbed a strand of her hair and ran it through his fingers. At last, he stood, reluctance in every inch of his body. "I need to get to *Onkel* Jed's *haus*."

She stood, too. "Someday soon, we won't have to say goodbye."

"*Jah*. That is true. Tomorrow will you come with me to talk with my parents?"

She nodded. "We can take my car to make the journey quicker."

At the door, Luke turned to her again and drew a finger down her cheek. "I love you. Until tomorrow."

She nodded. He leaned in and kissed her softly before slipping away into the night.

She shut the door and rested against it, closing her

eyes to hold close to her heart the memory of the way he looked at her. It was really happening. He loved her, and soon, they'd be a family, this time for good.

Sometimes dreams did come true.

She opened her eyes. She'd been in the process of taking the tree down when he'd shown up at her door. It seemed strange to think that just a few hours ago, the coming year had seemed so bleak. Now it was teeming with hope and wonderful possibilities.

All the weariness from earlier had faded. She had so much to do tomorrow.

She peeked in on LJ. He was sleeping, his teddy bear close in his arms. He'd kicked off his blanket in his sleep. She bent and kissed his soft head. He didn't even stir.

"Sleep well, LJ." She pulled the covers up over him. "Tomorrow, we're going home."

She didn't know exactly where they'd end up. It didn't matter. Home would be where they could be together.

A family, at last.

EPILOGUE

Jennie heard a deep chuckle behind her as she dropped her hammer—for the third time. Startled, the nail she'd been holding fell from her fingers and skittered across the plywood floor.

Luke strode farther into the room and stooped to pick up the nail. He flashed her a grin, humor dancing in his eyes. "I guess I should pick it up for you, since I'm the reason you dropped it."

"Yeah, you should." She propped a hand on her hips but couldn't maintain her outraged posture for too long. Too much joy was soaring through her body today.

"*Ach*, Jennie girl, this *haus* will never be ready in time for the Hoppers to move in if you keep dropping hammers and losing nails," *Onkel* Jed called out from the door.

She didn't take him too seriously. Not when she could clearly see the shine of his grinning teeth tucked inside of his long gray beard.

He continued, "Maybe we ought to put you back on painting detail, like we did back when you were a *kind*."

She snorted, but then ruined it by laughing at herself. They did have a point. Truth be told, she preferred painting, anyway. "You could be right."

"He is not," Luke asserted. "I think you've been a huge help."

"That's only because you like having your *frau* by your side all the time." Raymond sauntered into the room. His own beard was starting to come in.

Jennie and Luke had been together as husband and wife for nearly six months. She'd had to take the time to learn about the Amish and join the church. Once she did, Luke had made short work of going through an Amish wedding ceremony. They had attended Raymond's wedding to Mary Ellen last month.

Jennie loved having a large family around her. And it was made even better knowing that Aiden and his family were welcome to visit.

Aiden and Luke had hit it off immediately. Of course, her older brother was bound to approve of any man that risked his own life to protect Jennie and LJ.

"Let's take a break," *Onkel* Jed called out. "It's lunchtime."

Luke walked over and put his hands around Jennie's waist, lifting her off her ladder and setting her to the ground. Jennie squealed in surprise. He smiled, and if his hands lingered on her waist a moment longer than necessary, no one seemed to notice.

Hand in hand, they walked outside to where the other workers were coming to join them. LJ ran over to her side. She couldn't help the smile that stretched across her face as her little man scooted in between her and Luke. He was adorable in his dark trousers and straw hat. A perfect little Amish boy. He peeked up at Luke and tried to match his expression and stance. It warmed her heart to see LJ try to emulate his father.

She didn't blame him. She couldn't think of a single

man who was more admirable than her beloved husband. In her mind, he was everything a husband and father should be. Caring, strong and, most important, he put God first, always.

"Do you ever regret moving back to this part of the state?" she asked Luke softly as they were making their way back to their own house. They'd danced around the subject several times, but she'd never gotten up the courage to ask. Maybe because she wasn't sure she wanted to hear the answer. And Luke would never lie to her, not even if he thought his answer would upset her.

She peeked in the back. The sway of the buggy had already lulled LJ off to sleep. He'd played hard all day with the other children. After the terrifying time they'd spent when Steve was after them, he'd had nightmares for several months. Plus, he'd become overly clingy. All she had to do was step out of the room, and he'd start shrieking her name. Nearly a year later, seeing him laugh without fear and watching him go off to play without glancing back over his shoulder was a huge relief.

Luke patted her hand with his before putting it back on the reins. "I don't regret it. My *mamm* and *daed* are fine. Simon took over the *haus* when they moved in the *dawdi haus*, and they have the grandchildren to keep them busy."

She nodded. "I know. I just worry because both you and Raymond moved to Meadville to work with *Onkel* Jed. I hope they don't blame me." There. It was out. She'd finally said what had really bothered her.

She didn't think they did. But it still concerned her.

"*Nee*, don't you worry, Jennie. *Mamm* and *Daed* love you, they do. And LJ, too." He steered the mare left to go down their road.

The scent of dust caught her nostrils. She was beginning to enjoy the smell because it meant home.

"They always knew that I didn't belong in New Wilmington," he went on. "When I had come back, they were just relieved that I was Amish again. When you and I moved here, they didn't need to worry that I would be drawn to the *Englisch* way of life. My heart was completely taken up with you and our son."

Sighing, she leaned her head against his strong shoulder, feeling his muscles move as he continued to direct the mare into their driveway.

"Don't forget your mission work."

"*Jah.* That was the work *Gott* put on my heart. They would never fight against His will. The fact that I am able to do *Gott*'s work with my wife and my son, not to mention my closest brother, at my side, well, that is a great blessing in my life."

He stopped the buggy to let her off at the side porch. She gathered LJ into her arms.

"Do you need me to carry him?" he whispered.

She shook her head. "Nah. He's soon going to be too big for me, but I can still handle him."

She'd miss it when she could no longer carry her boy. A smirk edged onto her face. Although, there would be others. Very soon.

When Luke came in for the night, she watched him as he hung his hat by the back door. There was still light coming in the front windows, although it was fading fast.

"Want to watch the sunset?" she asked.

In response, he laced his fingers with hers and opened the front door. They stepped out onto the porch. She inhaled deeply. The lilacs were fragrant this evening.

Luke stepped behind her and wrapped his arms around her middle. His chin rested on her white *kapp*. She sighed, content.

"Hey, Luke?"

"Hmm?"

"I've been thinking about what we were talking about earlier. You know, about how LJ is going to be too big for me to carry soon."

"Jah?" He kissed the top of her head. She could feel the warmth through her *kapp*. How she loved this man!

"Well, I think that I'm going to have to stop carrying him in about three months."

"Huh?" He moved his arms and came to stand beside her. "What does three months have to do with it? We have no way of knowing how much he'll grow in that time."

"True." She ducked her head to hide the grin threatening to break loose. "However, I'll be too big probably."

She let that sentence settle into the silence between them. The expectancy in the air was almost tangible.

After about thirty seconds, she dared to peep up at Luke. His eyes were wide and glistening. Seeing him so close to tears, she had to fight back her own.

"Jennie? Are you?" His voice was hoarse.

She nodded. "I am. Nearly two months along."

He shook his head even as a smile bloomed across his face. A tear tracked down his cheek, but he didn't appear to be aware of it. His right hand moved to rest across her belly. "A *boppli*."

"Yes, we're going to have a baby."

"I never got to see LJ as a baby."

That nearly broke her heart. "I know. But you'll see

this one, every step of the way. And LJ will be such a great big brother."

They stood for a few minutes in silence, just happy to be in each other's presence. Suddenly, Luke was half laughing, half growling.

"What?"

He stood back to stare into her face. "I'm so happy about this, all I want to do is go to tell Raymond, and my *onkel* and everyone the news. But it's not the Amish way."

Jennie bit her lip. She remembered his cousin had had a baby a month ago. She'd suspected the woman was carrying, but no one had said anything until the baby was actually born. Even the brothers and sisters weren't told. "Okay, I know it's not the Amish way, but I really want to tell Aiden and Sophie."

"Of course! That should be fine. They're not Amish. I don't expect they'll be telling anyone around here."

When he held out his arms, she slipped into them. Tilting her head back so she could peer up into his face, she smiled. "God has blessed us so much, Luke. I don't have the words to say how happy I am at this moment. Or to say how very much I love you."

"Who needs words?" Her husband bent his head to kiss her, showing her without words that he, too, loved her beyond words.

* * * * *

Dear Reader,

Thank you for taking the time to read *Deadly Amish Reunion*. I hope that you fell in love with Jennie and Luke and, of course, LJ the way I did.

I have loved reading reunion romances ever since I first started reading romances as a teenager. Seeing couples who were once parted get a second chance at happy-ever-after never fails to move me. I love watching them overcome whatever obstacles separated them in the first place.

When I started to write books with Amish characters in 2016, I knew I wanted to have a story where one character was Amish and the other wasn't. The fact that Luke and Jennie were married with a child produced its own challenges! Challenges they were able to overcome through their faith in God and love for each other.

I love to hear from readers! You can find me on Facebook, Twitter, Instagram and on my website, www.danarlynn.com.

Blessings,
Dana R. Lynn

COMING NEXT MONTH FROM
Love Inspired Suspense

Available January 1, 2021

DESERT RESCUE
K-9 Search and Rescue • by Lisa Phillips

Search and Rescue K-9 handler Patrick Sanders is dispatched to find tw
kidnap victims in his hometown: his high school love, Jennie, and the so
he never knew existed. When Jennie escapes and runs right into him, ca
they work together with Patrick's furry partner to shield their little boy?

ON THE RUN
Emergency Responders • by Valerie Hansen

When a gang of criminals charge into an ER, they force nurse
Janie Kirkpatrick to treat the gunshot wound of one of their men. But
after things go bad, the leader vows to kill Janie, and her only hope of
survival is going on the run with undercover cop Brad Benton.

SEEKING AMISH SHELTER
by Alison Stone

Stumbling upon illegal drug activity in the health care clinic where she
works thrusts nursing student Bridget Miller into the crosshairs of a
violent criminal. Now under the protection of DEA Agent Zachary Bryant
she has no choice but to hide in the Amish community she left behind.

ALASKA SECRETS
by Sarah Varland

When her first love, Seth Connors, is attacked, former police officer
Ellie Hardison knows the crime is linked to his sister's death. To find the
culprits, she and Seth must go undercover on a dog-mushing expedition
but can they live long enough to find the truth?

TEXAS WITNESS THREAT
by Cate Nolan

Assistant US attorney Christine Davis is positive she witnessed a murde
but with no body at the scene, the police aren't convinced. Now someo
wants her dead, and Texas Ranger Blake Larsen is the only one who
believes her. But can he keep her safe from an unknown enemy?

CRIME SCENE CONNECTION
by Deena Alexander

A serial killer is imitating the murders from Addison Keller's bestselling
novel, determined to make her the final victim. But with former police
officer Jace Montana's help, Addison might just be able to unmask the
murderer...and escape with her life.

Get 4 FREE REWARDS!

We'll send you 2 FREE Books plus 2 FREE Mystery Gifts.

Love Inspired Suspense books showcase how courage and optimism unite in stories of faith and love in the face of danger.

FREE Value Over **$20**

YES! Please send me 2 FREE Love Inspired Suspense novels and my 2 FREE mystery gifts (gifts are worth about $10 retail). After receiving them, if I don't wish to receive any more books, I can return the shipping statement marked "cancel." If I don't cancel, I will receive 6 brand-new novels every month and be billed just $5.24 each for the regular-print edition or $5.99 each for the larger-print edition in the U.S., or $5.74 each for the regular-print edition or $6.24 each for the larger-print edition in Canada. That's a savings of at least 13% off the cover price. It's quite a bargain! Shipping and handling is just 50¢ per book in the U.S. and $1.25 per book in Canada.* I understand that accepting the 2 free books and gifts places me under no obligation to buy anything. I can always return a shipment and cancel at any time. The free books and gifts are mine to keep no matter what I decide.

Choose one: ☐ **Love Inspired Suspense Regular-Print** (153/353 IDN GNWN)   ☐ **Love Inspired Suspense Larger-Print** (107/307 IDN GNWN)

Name (please print)

Address   Apt. #

City   State/Province   Zip/Postal Code

Email: Please check this box ☐ if you would like to receive newsletters and promotional emails from Harlequin Enterprises ULC and its affiliates. You can unsubscribe anytime.

Mail to the **Reader Service**:
IN U.S.A.: P.O. Box 1341, Buffalo, NY 14240-8531
IN CANADA: P.O. Box 603, Fort Erie, Ontario L2A 5X3

Want to try 2 free books from another series? Call 1-800-873-8635 or visit www.ReaderService.com.

*Terms and prices subject to change without notice. Prices do not include sales taxes, which will be charged (if applicable) based on your state or country of residence. Canadian residents will be charged applicable taxes. Offer not valid in Quebec. This offer is limited to one order per household. Books received may not be as shown. Not valid for current subscribers to Love Inspired Suspense books. All orders subject to approval. Credit or debit balances in a customer's account(s) may be offset by any other outstanding balance owed by or to the customer. Please allow 4 to 6 weeks for delivery. Offer available while quantities last.

Your Privacy—Your information is being collected by Harlequin Enterprises ULC, operating as Reader Service. For a complete summary of the information we collect, how we use this information and to whom it is disclosed, please visit our privacy notice located at corporate.harlequin.com/privacy-notice. From time to time we may also exchange your personal information with reputable third parties. If you wish to opt out of this sharing of your personal information, please visit readerservice.com/consumerschoice or call 1-800-873-8635. **Notice to California Residents**—Under California law, you have specific rights to control and access your data. For more information on these rights and how to exercise them, visit corporate.harlequin.com/california-privacy.

LIS20R2

SPECIAL EXCERPT FROM

LOVE INSPIRED SUSPENSE
INSPIRATIONAL ROMANCE

*With his K-9's help, search and rescue K-9 handler
Patrick Sanders must find his kidnapped secret child.*

Read on for a sneak preview of
Desert Rescue *by Lisa Phillips,*
available January 2021 from Love Inspired Suspense.

"Mom!"

That had been a child's cry. State police officer Patrick
Sanders glanced across the open desert at the base of a
mountain.

Had he found what he was looking for?

Tucker sniffed, nose turned to the breeze.

Patrick's K-9 partner, an Airedale terrier he'd gotten
from a shelter as a puppy and trained, scented the wind.
His body stiffened and he leaned forward. As an air-scent
dog, Tucker didn't need a trail to follow. He could catch
the scent he was looking for on the wind or, in this case,
the winter breeze rolling over the mountain.

Patrick's mountains, the place he'd grown up. Until
right before his high school graduation when his mom
had packed them up and fled town. They'd lost their
home and everything they'd had there.

Including the girl Patrick had loved.

He heard another cry. Stifled by something—it was
hard to hear as it drifted across so much open terrain.

He and his K-9 had been dispatched to find Jennie
her son, Nathan. A friend had reported them missing
terday, and the sheriff wasted no time at all calling for
arch and rescue team from state police.

The dog had caught a scent and was closing in.

As a terrier, it was about the challenge. Tucker had
ved to be both prey-driven, like fetching a ball, and
d-driven, like a nice piece of chicken, when he felt
it.

Right now the dog had to find Jennie and the boy so
rick could transport them to safety. Then he intended
get out of town again. Back to his life in Albuquerque
studying for the sergeant's exam.

Tucker tugged harder on the leash; a signal the scent
stronger. He was closing in. Patrick's night of
rching for the missing woman and her child would
n be over.

Tucker rounded a sagebrush and sat.

"Good boy. Yes, you are." Patrick let the leash slacken
ttle. He circled his dog and found Jennie lying on the
und.

"Jennie."

She stirred. Her eyes flashed open and she cried out.
e need to find Nate."

Don't miss
Desert Rescue *by Lisa Phillips,*
*available wherever Love Inspired Suspense books
and ebooks are sold.*

LoveInspired.com

LOVE INSPIRED

INSPIRATIONAL ROMANCE

UPLIFTING STORIES OF FAITH, FORGIVENESS AND HOPE.

Join our social communities to connect with other readers who share your love!

Sign up for the Love Inspired newsletter at **LoveInspired.com** to be the first to find out about upcoming titles, special promotions and exclusive content.

CONNECT WITH US AT:

HARLEQUIN

Heartfelt or suspenseful, inspiring or passionate, Harlequin has your happily-ever-after.

With new books published every month, you are sure to find the satisfying escape you know you deserve.